This novel is dedicated to those who bravely face the daily battles of chronic illness and mental health conditions, and to the cherished souls who have fought with all their strength but are no longer with us. Your courage and resilience inspire every page.

THE OTHER SIDE OF THE BUTTERFLY

BUTTERFLY

C. HELEN

ISBN 978-1-9191982-0-0 (paperback 1st edition)
ISBN 978-1-9191982-1-7 (ebook 1st edition)

PROLOGUE
BELLA HOLTON

July 2008

"Bella, love, I am going to look like a flipping snowman before you're done," Jim said, tapping his fingers impatiently on his wheelchair's armrest as I applied another layer of factor fifty sun cream on his handsome face.

"Stop ya fussing, Jim. I've heard about those sun diseases on TV, and there is no way I am letting you get one of those. Do you hear me?"

It still surprises me, after all these years, how much he can make me go weak at the knees. Especially when he raises one of his bushy, grey eyebrows and gives me a cheeky wink.

I pushed Jim's wheelchair down to our family's sizeable beach huts, jointly owned with the Braxtons.

My nephew and his wife, Austin and Sally Holton, had argued with the council for months to get them to put a disabled ramp down on Whitebridge Sands. I was so glad they'd succeeded. Have you ever tried pushing a wheelchair on the sand without one? Impossible, I tell you.

The new ramps made such a difference. We could go to our lovely beach huts and down to a section of the sea.

I parked Jim next to the first beach hut. It had a white roof and was freshly painted in a boring duck-egg blue. We Holtons oversaw the maintenance of this beach hut, and the Braxtons oversaw the beach hut next door – painted in baby pink in its entirety. It even had adorable stars painted on it. I requested a similar theme to the Braxtons', yet sadly, I was outvoted.

"Move me around so I can see how to best organise this operation," Jim said.

"Yes, sergeant!" I manoeuvred Jim into place a few feet away from the beach hut door, then unlocked the heavy-duty padlocks and had a peek inside.

"The majority must be in the Braxtons' hut, darling. Only a few boxes here," I called.

I felt a sharp slap on my bottom and gasped.

"Jim! The doctor said for you not to propel the wheelchair. Conserve your energy."

"The doctor tells me not to do many things. Now, close that door and bring that magnificent arse back over here!" Jim kissed the back of my hand while keeping his eyes firmly focused on me.

I playfully slapped his arm. "We can't, darling. The family will be here soon, and how would we even do the hanky-panky in here?"

Suddenly, I felt foolish in my lengthy diamanté dress – the weather was far too hot for such an outfit. Not long after Jim received his diagnosis, he said we'd never leave anything for the best, including our clothes.

"No time like the present, love. Shut the door, and I will show you the rest." Jim raised both his eyebrows.

I giggled like a schoolgirl and quickly rushed to shut the door.

We were interrupted a lot earlier than we'd expected. The problem was the beach hut doors. They weren't lockable from the inside. Trying to stop someone from coming in, even when they were carrying a cardboard box of beach toys, was futile.

"Bella, what on earth are you doing? You will break a hip with that sort of thing. This is a family place, not a place to practise your exotic activities. Isn't that right, George?" Ida said, her tight, silver curls barely moving as she shook her head in disbelief.

I quickly made myself and Jim decent, yet I couldn't help but smile at our mischief, plus I love seeing my Jim so full of life.

"Yes, dear." George, who had a permanently miserable face, dutifully agreed and looked down at the floor.

"Ida, maybe you should practise some exotic activities. It would probably make your George crack a smile," Jim said. We both attempted to disguise our amusement, but we burst into uncontrollable laughter anyway.

"Filth! Come on, George, I have heard enough of this."

George followed Ida like a lost sheep to the next beach hut.

"Come on, you, we'd better help out before everyone is in a mood with us." I kissed my husband on his flushed cheek and pushed him back into the sunshine.

"Ah, forget about them. I am in a great mood."

"Yes, I bet you are!"

We both chuckled.

~

Everyone had arrived, and the sunny weather was breathtaking, and the salty sea air, refreshing. The beachside table and chairs were set up, the huge umbrella open, and we had a delicious array of picnic food available to us all. Of course, my baking took centre stage and was already a favourite. More favourable than Ida's cheese salad and hummus. Yuk!

"Oh, Bella, you've outdone yourself. Your Victoria sponge cake is even better than last time," James said.

"Yes, one hundred percent!" said Austin, sticking his finger into the cream of the fluffy sponge.

"How is Diane, James? I am sorry to hear she was not able to make it again. Are you alright? You keep looking at the trees over there. No monkeys in there, I'm afraid."

"Sorry, Bella. Yes, I'm fine. In fact, we're both fine. Just taking in the beautiful scenery. It never gets old." James gave me a faint smile, which disappeared almost immediately.

"How can you possibly eat all that in this scorching heat?" Ida tutted and fanned herself with her *Take a Break* magazine.

My spirit lifted as I saw Frank and Melody running up towards us, both wet through and covered in sand.

Feeling Melody's dripping-wet cotton cardigan, James said, "Duck, you need to take those clothes off, or you'll catch your death walking around in them. If you walk up the road to where your grandparents' caravan park used to be, there's a cheap clothes shop."

"Yes, they know us in there. Tell them you're Ida and George's granddaughter. They'll give you a good discount."

"Thank you, but these will dry." Melody moved closer to the picnic table, drooling over my delicious cake.

"Oh yeah! Aunt Bella's Victoria sponge."

Frank leaned over the table and grabbed two huge slices of cake, then kissed me on the cheek. *I love that boy.* I couldn't believe he was seventeen years old. He was such a handsome young man. Not being blessed with children myself, I tried not to impose my ideas onto parents, but I felt they'd missed so much of their precious boy's childhood due to that bloody hotel.

Still busy eating cake, Melody and Frank looked at each other like they were the best thing since sliced bread.

"Do you still love our feline friends?" I asked.

"Yes," Melody said. "I love cats. I'd like to volunteer with a cat rescue or something like that." She smiled, trying to hide behind Frank.

Jim turned to Melody. "Well, you're in luck. We now have a cat sanctuary at our house. I wanted to make my wife's dream come true, so I did." He kissed my hand, and we briefly exchanged a loving look.

"So, whenever you have time in your school holidays, you are more than welcome to stay with us and be our lead cat carer," I announced.

"That sounds amazing! Thank you so much."

"And we can spend more time together," Frank said.

Frank and Melody hugged each other closely and did a little happy dance.

"Well, you can spend time with Melody when you are not working at the hotel, son," Sally mumbled.

"Aunt Bella, I have learned some great new photography skills. Can I show you?" he asked. He took another bite of cake and reached for his expensive camera with his free hand, placing it in front of me.

"Of course you can." He had a born talent for this sort of thing, and his whole being lit up.

"I wish you wouldn't encourage him, Bella," Sally said.

"Rubbish, why can't the poor lad be excited about his passion? He wants to live and spread his wings like those unicorns." I sipped my tea and felt my hand gently being held by my Jim.

"Leave it, love," he whispered.

"He doesn't have time for hobbies. You know very well we need to prepare him for his future." Sally stared daggers at both me and Frank, who had started to put his fancy camera away in its case. Frank's bubble had been burst once again by his mother, and by gum, I was not letting her ruin my boy's day.

"Bella has never run a proper business, Sally, so she'll never understand," Ida said.

I stood up and clapped my hands. "Don't you dare put that camera away. I want some photos of me looking gorgeous by the sea! You too, Melody. Let's go find your sister as well."

Frank and Melody attempted to hide a smile. Frank excitedly got his camera ready, with Melody still stuck to him like glue.

Sally folded her arms and looked away from me. Austin was attempting to block out everything. He certainly agreed with Sally, but wasn't one for drama, so he focused on his newspaper.

"I am going to have a nap while you're gone, love. Cake coma." Jim chuckled, his eyes already closed.

"Grace is over there on that purple blanket." James pointed to the right of us, though he was still staring into the trees with a deep frown.

"Grace, why are you sat over here all by yourself?" Grace looked immaculate, as always. She was wearing a long navy summer dress, and her glossy hair framed her face perfectly.

"Aunt Bella! Sorry, I was zoned in my book." Grace gave me a loving hug while still holding on to her book. I felt such warmth from her embrace.

Frank said, "Will you look after my camera, please, Aunt Bella?" Before I could answer, he'd put it in my hand. He and Melody ran over to where Grace sat and leaped to sit beside her like they were on a trampoline. *Oh, to have that flexibility again.*

"Snooze cruise, Grace. Come on, have some fun with us." Frank snatched Grace's book and stuffed it up the front of his damp T-shirt.

Grace launched at Frank, but he quickly rolled away, getting closer to the sea. Melody followed Frank, also rolling down the sand – and ended up drenched, again.

"Frank, give me my book back now! I need to study. It's important," Grace shouted.

"If you don't agree to have fun with us, I'm rolling myself into the sea right now."

Grace ran straight for Frank, sand going everywhere from the speed of her feet. Reaching him, she attempted to take her book back, but to no avail. Frank threw the textbook a good way from the sea up onto the beach.

Then Melody and Frank playfully dragged a reluctant Grace into the sea. Their laughter was so loud, I was sure the entire beach could hear them.

Things started to settle down, and Frank came bounding over the sand towards me. Taking his camera from me, he said, "I have an amazing idea! Aunt Bella, can you help me get everyone to come together around here?" Frank marked a spot in the sand about five metres away.

"We need to do it now, while the lighting is perfect. Please, Aunt Bella, you are the only one who can whip everyone into shape." *Well, he is right there*, I thought.

Frank got on with organising us for the group shot, having already set up his tripod. James and Austin lifted my Jim and his wheelchair over to the spot to enable him to be in the photo as well. Melody was attempting to hide her body behind Grace, and Grace was clinging to her slightly damp book. I was standing by James and my Jim, blowing a kiss into the camera, and I could feel Ida's eyes burning into the back of my head. We had the sandy beach beneath our feet and, in the background, the small woodland on a slight hill. *My boy knows how to take a great photo!*

Everybody was standing in place, waiting for Frank.

"OK, everyone, I have put the camera on a ten-second timer, so don't move – and do your best pose." Frank ran back to take his place in the group, next to Melody, who was standing beside Grace.

James twisted his head around to look at the group of trees, and I followed his gaze. A mixture of greens as the sunlight shone through the trees. Glorious. Wait—

That was not what he was looking at. In fact, he was staring at a woman in a chestnut-brown mini dress who was trying to disguise herself within the trees. She was gawking at James with great intensity.

"Bella, you know nothing. Please, for the sake of my girls," James whispered, holding his body rigid, as if it would snap at any minute.

The blinding flash of the camera refocused my attention momentarily.

"OK, great! Let's just get a couple more to make sure," Frank said.

I turned to look again, but the mysterious woman had gone.

"I really don't know anything, James, but now I am concerned about you and your girls."

1

MELODY BRAXTON

JANUARY 2017

Emma pushed past me, stomping off towards dad's black Honda Jazz in a rush. She climbed in and slammed the door behind her. There was an aura of bitterness around Emma, and it spread to everyone she met.

Dad rolled his eyes and sighed before getting into the driver's seat.

My chest tightened, and I remembered to take slow breaths as I opened the rear door and got in.

We set off and I wound the window down. Sitting in silence, I began to enjoy the refreshing, cool breeze on my skin. The air was crisp, and I was hypnotised by the clear blue sky.

"You can nip to the video game store, duck, and get that game you want for your birthday," Dad said.

I smiled as a feeling of relief rushed through my body.

"Thanks, Dad! I thought everyone had forgotten."

Emma twisted her body around to glower directly at me. "Do you think you really deserve a birthday gift? When you have done fuck all."

"Emma! Just shut up, will you? I have really had enough

of your crap today, and Melody has been working with me," Dad said.

"Are you having a laugh? She moved a few boxes and spends the rest of the time on her bloody phone. Leaving you to do the work of two people."

"Emma, leave her alone!"

Emma scowled as she turned to face the front. She folded her arms, and my muscles relaxed with the relief that I didn't have to face her judgemental eyes for the rest of the journey.

We parked next to North Litten Library, a library surrounded by a beautiful park, where there are lots of wooden benches and stunning flowers with powerful but pleasant aromas. Grace and I had probably sat on every bench, chatting about the books we'd read. We used to come here when we were younger, always excited to borrow more books. I loved picking what adventure to go on next, but there were so many to choose from.

I climbed out of the car. Staring at the library's welcoming entrance, I smiled, hopeful that maybe Grace and I would come back again one day.

"Right then, Mel, shall we pop into town and leave mardy arse in the car?" Dad grinned. He got out of the car and shut his door before Emma had the chance to speak.

I'd lived in North Litten all my life, but still felt my heart pounding as we walked along the cobbled streets. Leaving the comfort zone of my home was always difficult. Yet, the sun's warmth on our faces was truly welcoming, especially for January. The nice weather reminded me of my grandparents, who immigrated to Spain several years ago.

"Dad, when was the last time you heard from Grandma Ida and Grandad George?"

"Not for a while. I've been trying to call them, but it seems their phone is cut off. I've even sent them a few letters. They've never used email or anything like that. I'm worried, to be honest, Mel. I know they miss the caravan park, but they have been in Spain a long time now. I don't know...but I am sure they're fine." Dad looked off into the distance with his hands stuffed into his jeans pocket.

We stepped into the Georgian market square surrounded by magnificent period buildings, today full of families shopping and traders shouting about their goods, touting for business. Wiping my clammy hands on my top, I was distracted by a bellowing voice.

"Five bananas for a pound!" a market trader with tattered, fingerless gloves yelled close to my ear.

Startled, I stepped backwards, treading on Dad's toes.

"Oh blimey, are you OK? We'll just get a few things. We can always get the rest another day."

"Thanks, Dad. Shall we go to Game?"

"Tell you what, you go in there while I nip into B&Q, then I'll meet you back at the car in fifteen minutes?" Dad suggested.

A lump rose in my throat, but I nodded, trying to smile.

Rushing down one of the back streets, I kept my eyes focused on the ground. I didn't want to see people's reactions to my ugliness.

With my game in hand, I found a quiet corner in a back street. I messaged Frank to tell him I'd got the new *Call of Duty*, and now I could defeat him. I laughed to myself, knowing he would be practising his fighting talk.

The smell of traditional British burgers and hot dogs

wafted across the hectic marketplace. I hurried to the safety of Dad's car.

But at the end of the market, I froze on the spot. It felt like someone had poured a huge bucket of glue over my entire body. The sight in front of me broke my heart, and I couldn't even breathe.

He was standing there, wearing the violet Ted Baker shirt I bought him on our first anniversary. His soft, grey hair, which I always found sexy, was blowing in the wind, and I remembered all the times I'd run my hands through it. A stunning woman was attached to him, his arm wrapped around her. Her modelesque body snuggled into his middle-aged spread. I would have given anything to swap places with her.

Still, I was not stupid. No man would exchange the likes of me for a woman of their fantasies. The man I loved turned his face to meet hers, and they kissed passionately.

I doubled over, violently sick, throwing up my breakfast all over an empty market stall. I had to cling to the wooden posts for support. An unsightly scene of digested tomatoes, toast, and eggs dripped to the floor.

"That's disgusting! Tramp!" A small group of teenagers sniggered and pointed at my pathetic state.

Tears streamed down my face, and my feet barely touched the ground as I ran to Dad's car.

"Bloody hell, Mel, what in the world has happened?"

Dad held me as I wailed uncontrollably.

"You're making a scene, Melody, and you stink!" Emma said, turning her nose up as she leaned on the passenger door.

"Let's all get in the car, and please, Emma, just keep your comments to yourself."

Dad guided me into the back.

"Come on, James, even you can see this is not how an adult should behave." Emma pointed towards me as she got in the front.

Dad walked around the car and climbed in next to me. He held my sweaty hands.

"Dad! He's got another girlfriend. He doesn't love me anymore. The woman is like a model. She is perfect, and I still love him, and my heart hurts so bad," I bawled.

"For fucks' sake, Melody, what do you expect from dating a dirty old man?" Emma laughed.

"Emma, just shut up!" Dad shouted and thumped the back of Emma's car seat.

"Let's take a few deep breaths, Mel. I think it's best you try and have a fresh start now, putting the past behind you. One day at a time. We will get through this together."

Dad kissed me gently on my forehead. When he moved to get out, I grabbed his colourful woolly jumper. He turned back to look at me, his eyes full of concern.

"How do I get him back?" I whispered.

2

MELODY BRAXTON

JANUARY 2017

As I stepped out of the car, the smell of freshly cut grass hit me. Dad struggled to get his keys from his trouser pocket, and Emma was tapping her fingernails on the car bonnet.

"Come on, James. I want to have at least some time in my living room!" she said, scowling.

Dad completely ignored Emma's comment, and I stood, calming myself by staring at the bungalow – quaint, with four hanging baskets of assorted summer plants, and everywhere looked freshly painted. Emma was always making beautiful improvements to our family home. For all Emma's faults, she certainly could keep a home looking nice, unlike our mother.

Dad finally opened the door, and we walked into the bungalow, following Emma, who rushed inside. I shut the white UPVC door with force, relieved when I locked it and had finally shut the awful world out. *No one is going to hurt me here. Well, apart from Emma – but Dad will protect me.*

"We have a surprise for you!" Dad said.

"Really?" I said.

He pointed me in the direction of Grace's room, following me closely. I pulled a hair bobble around my wrist so tightly that the blood circulation was reduced temporarily. My relationship with my sister was not what it used to be. There was always an elephant in the room.

Dad shuffled to the side of me and knocked on Grace's door.

"Grace, are you ready, duckie?"

"Yes, come in," Grace said faintly.

"Surprise!" Dad waved his large hands side to side.

My sister clapped her delicate hands, her face alight with a sincere smile.

From her bedside cabinet, Grace handed me a black cat-themed napkin filled with milk chocolate drops.

"This is so great, thank you." I forced a smile.

"Now then, you two! Let's get this party started. What do you think of the decorations, Melody?" Dad winked.

Grace's bedroom had a huge, sparkly Happy Birthday banner over the top of her bed. The floor was covered in black cat-themed balloons, and on the back of her door hung a matching themed curtain. Under her bedroom window stood a home-helper trolley that was full of my favourite food.

"This is great, thanks. So where can I even sit?" I took a deep breath, trying to drown my powerful emotions from rising.

"I am going to pretend you didn't say that, Melody. Here is our fourth guest. Hopefully she will bring a smile to your face." Dad tilted his head towards Grace's bedroom door.

"Oh, Milly, look at you in your cute birthday bandanna." I crouched down on the floor and greeted my feline friend. My heart lifted as she purred at my touch. I wanted to cuddle her like a teddy bear, but that would end in several scratch marks. "We were trying to find a party theme kit that was exactly like Milly. Sadly, we couldn't find an exact one, but this is pretty close, don't you think?" Grace explained while she attempted to hold up a matching paper plate. The plate wobbled slightly as she struggled to keep her arm up.

Grace looked up at me for help, but I turned away.

"Look at that cake. It's like a huge Milly face. Aunt Bella made it," Dad said.

I started to drool. A round black-velvet cake with blackcurrant fruit pastilles for eyes and liquorice chewy twisters for whiskers. Delicious. I always love Aunt Bella's cakes.

"Was there a card or gift from Grandma Ida and Grandad George?" I asked.

"No, and I still can't get hold of them," Dad said, looking away.

He grabbed a sizeable silver gift bag from the floor. From it, he drew a brown paper parcel, which he placed on Grace's bed.

"Oh yes, your gifts, Melody. I think the parcel on top is from Frank and Aunt Bella."

I rushed to grab the parcel and tore the wrapping apart. I must have looked like a cat trying to open the lid of a tub of catnip.

"I forgot to tell you as well, Mel – Aunt Bella wrote me a letter and she enclosed some photos of some of the gorgeous cats she is looking after. She thought you would like to see them. They are in the drawer next to me, when you have finished unwrapping." Grace smiled again, leaning her head back on her mountain of pillows.

"Yeah, OK," I mumbled.

I held up two cat-themed birthday cards and an *Everything You Ever Wanted to Know about Cats!* book collection. "I can't wait to read these!"

I stopped to give Dad a closer look, but his arms were folded, his eyes screwed up tight.

I felt like my heart stopped for a moment. My dad never got angry, not at me, anyway.

He said, "You've treated your sister like garbage today. Even though she is in so much pain, she is the main reason why this surprise has happened for you today. I am so disappointed in your behaviour."

"It doesn't matter, Dad," Grace whispered.

"Yes, it does. Why have you behaved like this, Melody?"

I took another long, deep breath, but I could no longer drown the rising tide of my disappointment.

"We have a large living room. Grace, couldn't you have done the big journey to that room so I could have at least been comfortable and not squashed to death in this room, which you already took from me when you moved in here? You get the luxury of being here all the time, watching TV or whatever, and not having any pressure on you like I do. It really is the least you could have done."

Dad's arm dropped to his side as he shook his head and frowned.

"Come on, Dad. Grace has always had her eyebrows trimmed and hair immaculate since we were teenagers. Yet since she has been *ill,* she looks like she's been through a hedge backwards several times. Why aren't you pressuring her?"

Grace turned away from us and curled up in a foetal position.

I felt a slight pang of guilt.

"Leave, Melody!" Dad commanded.

When we arrived home the next day after getting some shopping, Emma and Dad went inside, leaving me to collect the bags. I dragged them from the Honda towards the bungalow.

"Hello, love." The elderly gentleman waved to me from the bungalow next door. He was sitting in a deckchair, surrounded by creepy-looking gnomes.

I waved in reply.

"You never know what the weather will be like in Britain, do ya? I am making the most of it," he said.

Nodding a reply, I rushed into the house, not wanting to engage with him.

With all the shopping inside, I leaned against the door and pressed my hand to my chest, trying to calm my erratic breathing. The less time outside, the better.

In the living room, Dad and Emma sat on the small floral-patterned sofa, watching a sitcom on their widescreen television. Opposite the sofa was an unused fireplace, above which was an enormous professional photo of Emma in a seductive pose. It gave me the creeps. I launched myself onto the matching four-seater sofa, removed my battered trainers, and unhooked my bra from underneath my king-sized jumper. Sighing with relief, I tossed my bra randomly and stretched my legs over the entire length of the settee.

"Do make yourself comfortable, Melody!" Emma snarled.

My heart sank. My mind was always in constant overdrive, like an out-of-control Ferris wheel. I just wanted to block everything out of my mind.

"Melody, you know this is a living room, and your dad and I are still living in it! Be respectful, at least!"

"I don't have a room, Emma. The living room is also my bedroom, and we know why!"

"Yes, because you won't get off your fat arse and get a place of your own."

I looked over to Dad, who was rubbing his temples.

"I just wanted to settle for the night. It's been quite a big day," I mumbled, chewing my chapped lips.

"Yes, it has! Clean up your mess, Melody, and have a wash! This room smelled nice until you walked in." Emma scrunched up her nose.

Tears pricked my eyes.

"Dad?"

Dad wiped a layer of sweat from his brow.

"Emma, I am exhausted. Melody, this is a living room, and you do need to be respectful that we all use it. Emma, we all need to be flexible, so stop with your nasty comments. I am going to bed, and I suggest you come with me, Emma."

Dad slowly rose to a standing position, and salty tears ran down my cheek as he left without saying goodnight. Emma's glare burned into me for a few moments, then she rose from the sofa and strutted after my dad. Surely, he should have stuck up for me. I needed support from my family, not this crap. I thought Dad was going to continue to protect me. He promised he would after Mum died. I didn't understand what was going on. My head throbbed as I tried to untangle all the troubling thoughts in my mind.

My mobile phone pinged. I searched for it in my bag while removing items carelessly. Finding it, I quickly glanced at it, expecting a sales promotion. My heart stopped. Joy bubbled up inside me, and I kissed my phone. Even though it was an unknown number, I knew the message was from him!

Hi Baby, I am hoping this is still your numba, found it in old phone. I have missed my naughty secretary.
P xx

3

GRACE BRAXTON

JANUARY 2017

Instagram Message

Dear Tina,

I always look forward to your messages. Did you
enjoy your Christmas break? I bet all the children of
your class will be telling you what they got from
Santa! My GP advised me that I needed to seek coun-
selling for my health concerns, and as much as it
angers me that my symptoms are still being related
to the mind, I am willing to try anything to get my
old life back. I explained to Kerry (my counsellor)
that I feel like a burden to everyone around me. I see
myself as an elderly unwanted relative, and my
family are getting impatient, waiting for me to die. I
am used to being a professional who is independent
in every aspect of their life. Each day brought me new
thrilling challenges, and every night I was happy and
proud knowing that I had achieved my high expecta-
tions. Now, I am a sloth that requires support for the
most mundane tasks. Kerry suggested that I need to

test my body again. She kept using the expression, "If you don't use it, you lose it." She thinks that I need to trust that my body can take care of itself. It's just that I have lost confidence in my own body. Therefore, I need to change my thought patterns to change my behaviour. She reassures me that I have nothing to worry about, as there is nothing physically wrong with me. There IS something physically wrong with me, and there were so many times I bit my tongue till it bled during that conversation. Are counsellors even supposed to give advice? I am not one hundred percent sure. Love Grace xx

My thin fingers attempted to grab the towel rail as I plunged to the damp floor. The impact felt like I had fallen from a towering mountain. Pain shot up my spine, and I gritted my teeth to stop myself from screaming. The hot water was mostly only hitting the institutional shower chair, and I only felt a slight spray. My teeth chattered as I slowly rose, trying to pull myself up with my thin, weak arms, so that I could get to a kneeling position and get up from the floor.

"Oh my god, Grace! What have you done? Mia, come here, please!" Zoey shouted.

She quickly rushed over to me, turned the shower off, and placed several soft towels around my shaking body. Zoey knelt in front of me, the knees of her black trousers already becoming soaked. Her moss-green tunic, with its *Care 4 You* logo, had become a part of my daily life. Worn by the many people who cared for me.

"Grace, you don't have to prove anything to anyone. You are going to end up hurting yourself badly one of these days." Zoey's voice softened as she attempted to warm me by rubbing the towels up and down my arms.

Most of the other carers tended to rush. They didn't have a lot of time to chat – and couldn't spend extra time on the things you would do if you could do them yourself. Such as cleaning behind your ears. I understood that the carers had an extremely strict schedule, and the management barely gave them any time, yet Zoey genuinely appeared to care, and most importantly, she believed me.

"Anyone there?" Zoey asked, smiling. "Let's try and get you back on the shower chair. Can you get on your knees, Grace?" Zoey said, guiding me with her gloved hand.

I attempted to haul my body to the position needed, but each movement sent fireworks of pain throughout my entire body.

"I don't think I can do it – the pain's killing me." I closed my eyes, and a warm, salty tear slipped down my damp cheek, knowing what was coming next.

Emma walked into the bathroom in her latest designer tracksuit and glared at me.

"Oh great! Come on, Grace, just get up. I've got a lot on today."

"Emma, I need to call an ambulance because I am not able to get Grace off the floor. And, you know, we cannot lift service users. Listen, I am just going to get some pillows, blankets, and some clothes for Grace. She could be waiting a long time," Zoey explained.

Emma placed her toned arms on her hips.

"Grace, get up! I am not waiting in for an ambulance again, and I do not have time to do more laundry," Emma shouted.

Zoey sharply clicked her fingers to bring Mia, the other carer, into the moment. Mia had been standing idly watching. She attempted to get her phone from her trouser pocket, but she dropped it onto the bathroom floor.

"Mia, for goodness' sake, ring an ambulance now for Grace," Zoey said.

Emma flipped her short bob and stood firmly in front of Zoey.

"Excuse me, I just said..."

Zoey stepped closer to Emma and took a deep breath. "Grace is under our care, and I will not leave her like this. If you do not allow the appropriate steps to go ahead, then I will need to call my manager, and then they'll call the appropriate authorities. Please move out of my way so I can get Grace's things."

Emma's jaw dropped.

"What a load of bullshit! Fine, fine, I will stay in as bloody always," Emma shouted before stomping to another room.

I felt like I was sitting on a bed of cacti: no position felt comfortable. A ripple of fatigue hit, making me want to shut my eyes. However, the spasms of shooting pain kept them wide open – and kept me wide awake.

Zoey rushed into the bathroom with my bedroom pillows, blanket, and nightdress. She wrapped her hair in a messy bun and gave me a concerned smile. She delicately placed the plumped pillows behind my back, the knitted blanket behind my bony shoulders, and gently pulled an oversized nightdress over my head.

"Mia has rung for the ambulance, but they could be several hours away. The Wicked Witch of the East Midlands seems to be getting worse, Grace. Have you spoken to your dad about how bad she's getting?"

I'd come up with that nickname, and yes, it was especially appropriate.

"Well, sort of. I mean, he has so much on his plate, I don't like to bother him. I appreciate that it can't be easy looking after a disabled daughter…I suppose putting up with his mad missus is a small price to pay," I said, adding a half-hearted laugh.

Zoey looked to the floor as if she were searching for answers in the depths of the vinyl covering. As she turned to face me, a cloud of sadness passed over her features.

"I don't want to cause any trouble for you, Grace, but you shouldn't be treated like this. I've got to get going for the next service user, but I will be back at the bedtime call."

Many hours later, I was still extremely uncomfortable, sitting on the bathroom floor, and the pain had become so overwhelming that I was suffering tidal waves of nausea. The relaxing smell of lavender shower gel had disappeared and was replaced with an aroma of musty towels.

The doorbell rang, and Emma answered the door immediately.

"Finally, you're here. Make your way through to the bathroom. She is on the floor. Launched herself off the shower chair. She will not get up. She always wants attention, that girl. Right, now you two are here, can I get going?"

"Are you the only person at home with the patient?" the paramedic asked.

Emma raised her voice. "Yes. But I have been waiting for hours for you lot, and I need to get going."

"We would appreciate it if you would stay at the property until we have seen the patient and decided on the best outcome," the paramedic said.

"For fuck's sake!" Emma slammed the lounge door as she disappeared, leaving the paramedics to find their own way.

I was surprised the doors of the bungalow were still on their hinges with the number of times they'd been slammed.

Two female paramedics entered the bathroom. They were both chubby and looked like they could beat you in an arm wrestling match any day. Both had bob-style haircuts, but different shades of blonde. The paramedics stood together, side by side.

"Hello, my name is Fern, and this is my colleague, Eva. We have been asked to come and see you regarding a fall. Can I just check you are Grace Braxton?"

"Yes, I'm Grace."

I was wondering why they were just standing there looking like large tree trunks while it was obvious I was in a vast amount of pain.

"So, why can't you get up, hun? The stressed-out lady we just met assumed you launched yourself, and the diagnosis we have been given from the carers would not suggest any problems to this extent." Fern raised her untidy eyebrow in suspicion.

My hands were starting to shake with fury, and I attempted to hold back the tears as I said, "I am in agony. I have been on the bathroom floor for hours, and now I am getting an interrogation by the people who are supposed to help me. You may have little knowledge, or ignorance of my condition, but there is plenty of research to suggest that it does cause these awful symptoms, and I shouldn't have to stick up for myself while I am in agony and half naked on the bathroom floor!" Both paramedics rolled their eyes at each other and then stared directly towards me. My stomach was in knots.

Fern pointed her fat finger at me. "You know you are stopping someone from receiving a vital service, someone that could be dying?"

Eve turned her back on me. "Babe, there is no way we can

leave her there, no matter what we think. Isla will come down on us like a tonne of bricks again."

"Yeah, I'm sure Drama Queen would squeal as well," Fern said.

The throbbing agony continued to move throughout my body. I was soaked in dripping sweat as my body fought the urge to lose consciousness. But a raised voice drew my attention.

"What the hell is going on here? According to my neighbour, you have been here for twenty minutes. Why is my daughter still on the floor? She looks in terrible pain! You two look like you are having a right chit-chat!"

Eve and Fern nearly tripped over each other as Dad rushed to my side. The warmth of his sturdy hand provided me with instant hope. Fern attempted to tower over him, folding both of her chunky arms. "Mr Braxton, Grace is known to the ambulance service for her *falls,* and my colleagues have taken her to the hospital before, and they never find anything wrong with her. We are already overrun and understaffed as it is. Have you found her psychiatric help yet?"

They genuinely thought I was insane and doing all of this on purpose! They treated me like a joke.

"Have you two done any part of your job? Checked her blood pressure? Her oxygen levels? You know, the medical tests you are supposed to be trained to do?"

Rather than admit to their failings, they both stared directly at Dad and started to snigger.

Dad quickly rose to his feet and shooed the paramedic twins away.

"Get out! Get out! Get out of my house now! Your manager will know about this by the end of the day."

"Mr Braxton, we need you to sign this form to say—"

"Get out now!" Dad interrupted, shoving them out of the bathroom.

The next thing I heard was the slamming of our front door.

Dad carefully carried me to my bedroom. He held me delicately in a way a father would carry a baby. With the remaining strength I had left, I held on to his T-shirt and nestled my head into his chest. I felt instant relief as my body reached the comfort of my bed. My body was fire, and my inviting bed was the water.

Dad had large, sweaty patches under both of his arms. He fanned himself aggressively with one of my writing magazines.

"Dad, are you OK? Do you need a drink?" I noticed the bags under his eyes were darker than usual.

"Yeah, yeah fine...You must be starving, duckie. Let me get you some grub and your medication."

"Could I just have a drink and my medication, please? I am not hungry. But I am worried about you, Dad. Are you OK?"

"Yeah, I am fine. Where is Emma, by the way?"

"I don't know."

Dad left my bedroom, looking at his mobile phone. I attempted to drag my duvet towards me, yet it felt like it was stuck on some invisible hook.

I was still wrestling with it when Dad returned with my tray. Putting it down, he said, "What are you doing there, duckie?"

"My duvet's stuck on something."

Dad easily managed to free it, and I was grateful for the warm cocoon.

"Here's your favourite squash and your medication. I really hope they help you feel better, especially after this awful day. And don't you worry, I will be getting on to the ambulance management now."

Dad passed me my prescribed codeine and my drink. I was incredibly thirsty, and the blackcurrant tasted like the best thing I'd ever tasted.

"I almost forgot. This letter arrived for you today. Looks like Aunt Bella's writing." Dad took a folded brown envelope out of his jeans pocket and placed it in front of me. I loved receiving letters from Aunt Bella, but due to the over-whelming fatigue, I was unable to even focus my eyes on my name and address on the envelope.

"Thank you, Dad, but I am worried about you. Are you sure you're OK?"

"Stop worrying, please. Oh yeah, I also forgot to say, I left your sister sleeping in the van. We had a big clearance today, and she's out for the count. I didn't wake her because I rushed into the house as soon as I saw the ambulance."

Dad's phone vibrated, and he left my bedroom without looking up from his screen.

Milly, my sister's adorable jet-black cat, jumped up onto my bed and gracefully padded towards me. She nuzzled close to my face and provided me with a comforting purr.

"Things will get better soon, won't they, Milly?"

Meow.

4

MELODY BRAXTON

JANUARY 2017

After seeing Patrick the night before, I lay awake thinking about him, so I texted him around 2.00 a.m. I got no response at that time, so I expected to hear from him in the morning.

—Hi babe, Thank you so much for a wonderful evening. I can't wait to see you again. xxx

When I woke, there was still no reply from him, so I texted him again.

—Hi Babe, Have a good day at work. When can I see you again? Xxx

And still no reply by lunchtime. I was getting nervous. I needed him to get back to me.

—Is everything OK, babe? Xxx

The screen on my phone would not change, however

much I urged it to, even with my constant staring. My eyes became blurred. There were no notifications.

Thinking about it, even when we were in a relationship, he was not the best at replying to my messages. He used to tell me he was not one of those people who had their phone with them all the time.

Yet, last night his phone was in the car with us, and he checked it several times. I assumed he hadn't slept well and he was running late for work, which also made him miss his lunch break...maybe.

The previous night, as soon as I had climbed into his Mercedes-Benz sports car, he had hugged me tightly for several minutes, saying how much he'd missed me. Knowing I am not big on socialising, he thoughtfully suggested that we spend time together in his car in a secluded place. I love how he always smells of Old Spice and cigars, which sends erotic shivers down my spine.

After a few pleasurable hours together, he drove me home, and for the first time in a long while, I had a bouncy spring in my step. However, there were still so many unanswered questions that I was too nervous to ask. I didn't want him to freak out again.

∿

Frank messaged me to join him for a raid on one of our favourite video games. Our battles always helped take my mind off my ruminations, and Frank made me smile, no matter what was going on.

I went to turn on my console – but where was it? Panic rising, I scanned the living room. Then I jumped to my feet and rushed around the bungalow, searching all over.

"Where is my stuff?" I shouted at the top of my lungs. I pulled my hair bobbles tighter.

From the corner of my eye, I spotted three cardboard boxes in the corner of the kitchen. Upon closer examination, I saw words in black ink: 'Melody's Crap.'

"I really hate you, Emma," I mumbled.

I chucked everything out of the boxes onto the kitchen floor until I finally found my console, games, and accessories. At that moment, Milly decided to jump up on the kitchen table – and slipped on a couple of Emma's magazines next to a vase of flowers.

I reacted like a mother attending to a crying baby, grabbing my furry feline just in time to prevent her fall.

But the vase shattered, leaving broken glass on the floor.

"What are you doing, my little Milly?"

Milly struggled out of my arms, landing at my feet.

"We've made a mess, haven't we? Never mind. I'll clean up after the raid – I am already late. Come on, follow me. I don't want you going back in there."

Milly stretched and yawned before following me towards *Grace's* room.

"Can I come in?" I asked as I reached the door.

"Yes," Grace whispered.

I walked into *her* bedroom.

"I need to move more stuff into *your* room. Emma had my stuff boxed up in the kitchen, looking like it was ready for the tip, and I nearly missed another important raid..."

I stopped my rant and focused on her red face, swollen eyes, and the pile of tissues on her bed.

I didn't want to care; she just wanted attention.

"Put whatever you need into this room."

More tears fell onto her pale cheeks as she stared aimlessly at her wardrobe.

I walked closer to Grace's side.

"Don't cry, Grace. Everything will be OK."

She smiled up at me. For the first time in ages, we exchanged genuine smiles.

"I found this beautiful butterfly video on YouTube I thought you would like. Shall we watch it together?" I asked.

"Yes, I'd love that, Mel."

Grace slowly organised herself into a sitting position, pulling her butterfly pillows around her for support. Grace had always liked colourful butterflies, but even more so since she developed this mystery illness. Dad said her love of butterflies comes from our mother, but thinking about that makes me angry. Sitting next to my sister, we watched the video on my phone. The raid could wait.

I left Grace resting, and Milly zoomed past me before disappearing. I reached the kitchen doorway and shivered. Emma was lying on the marble kitchen floor, clutching her back, and her sister Joyce was kneeling beside her. I took a deep breath as they both directed their hateful eyes towards me.

"Have you seen what you have done? With all your crap on the floor? You are such a selfish child!" Joyce jabbed her manicured finger towards me.

My heart was pounding so loudly I could hear every beat. I went to help Emma get up off the floor, but she batted my hand away. I jolted backwards, stepping on the broken glass behind me, thankful I was wearing slippers.

"I am so sorry, Emma. I was just coming back...to clean this mess up," I stammered.

Joyce held her sister's hand as she supported her to a

kitchen chair. Emma landed heavily on the chair and cried out.

"Emma, would you like some painkillers, love? Have you got some paracetamols?"

My heart was beating so fast it felt like it would explode.

"Yes, there is some in the drawer over there." Emma pointed to the kitchen drawers.

Joyce grabbed the tablets and a bottle of water from the fridge.

According to the kitchen clock, I had been standing there for ten minutes. Yet, it felt like it'd been hours.

Joyce handed the tablets and water to her sister; I attempted to walk into the hallway.

"Wait! Where do you think you are going?" Joyce shouted.

I froze midway, one foot in the kitchen and one in the carpeted hallway.

"This is what I am talking about, Joyce. She never thinks of anyone else apart from herself, but she expects her father and I to look after her like she's a little girl. Are you not ashamed of the guilt trip you have put your father under, Melody? If not, then you bloody should be!"

I clenched my fists, then turned and marched back into the kitchen.

"How dare you! I have nothing to feel guilty for. I help in the house, and I go to work with Dad. What more do you expect from me? You are the one that keeps causing arguments and nastiness all the time."

My whole body trembled, and I bit my cheek to prevent the tears from coming.

The sisters cackled like old witches, clapping like they were giving me a round of applause.

"This is what I was telling you about, Joyce. She is so delusional, it's unreal."

"Melody, you are preventing your dad from hiring a full-time assistant who would actually do the job, not just move a few things, make cups of tea, then the rest of the time play on her phone. He actually needs assistance with his heavy manual job, but you don't care about that, do you?"

"That's not true! You are both so bitter. You knew when you married my dad that he had two daughters. If you wanted a man all to yourself, then you should have married someone with no kids!"

Joyce banged her fist on the kitchen table.

"You are an adult, Melody. You should be looking after yourself, plus on top of that, your dad promised Emma—"

"Joyce!" Emma interrupted.

"Promised Emma what?" My heart was beating faster by the second.

Joyce continued to glare at me.

"And by the way, I found out this morning that you went out with that dirty old man last night. So, explain this to me. Your dad works all the hours he can to keep you all going, Emma works non-stop to keep this gorgeous bungalow looking spotless, and on top of this she has to look after your crippled sister. Yet, you sit on your fat arse, watching TV or opening your legs for that creep of a boyfriend!" Joyce spat.

I gasped.

"Why is it always me you pick on? You never pick on Grace!" My voice started to break.

Like the pair of witches they were, they both cackled again.

"I think you are both retarded nutters," Emma said. "It's just that your sister got the ball rolling as soon as she moved in to make sure she paid at least some of her way. The majority of the benefits she receives goes to me and your dad and half of her PIP payment goes towards the carers' costs. Contribution payment, I think they call it."

Joyce continued. "You have been paid a full-time wage by your dad that you don't deserve. Yet you've not contributed to any of the household bills or food. And you make the most work in this home." She paused. "Melody, it's time for you to wake up. You are causing your dad so many problems, you disappoint him, and when your boyfriend finds out the truth about your laziness, he will want nothing to do with you, either."

I felt physically wounded by her words. Each word felt like a knife cutting into my heart, and the content was bleeding all over the floor. I was trying to help Dad. I thought I was of some use, especially as I could lift many of the heavy items on my own without any assistance. It was just that I had many mornings where I woke up in a cold sweat and struggled to calm my thoughts – and nothing seemed to stop my never-ending circle of terrifying emotions.

"Melody, we have an idea that might help us all out. Come and sit down." Emma pointed to the chair beside her.

I wanted to run away as far as possible. But was part of what they were saying true? Was I really that bad of a person that I was making my dad suffer? Would Patrick still want to see me if he knew everything?

I sat down next to Emma, and when Joyce joined us, an overpowering waft of sweat and musky body spray choked my senses.

Although I couldn't see them, I could feel their eyes boring into me as I sat staring at the floor. My left leg was tapping, and I continually twisted my hair bobble, trying not to make eye contact with either of them.

"My husband and I run several successful hairdressing salons across the East Midlands. We have won many awards, you know, been in many magazines for how amazing our salons are. When I advertise a job for one of our salons, we have like a thousand applications per job. We're so popular! Anyway, to cut to the chase, because Emma is my dear sister, I'm offering you an amazing opportunity to be a weekend assistant at our North Litten salon." Joyce smiled smugly and handed me a document. 'Joyce's Salons Employee Handbook.'

The document shook in my hands, and I couldn't control the tears rolling down my cheeks anymore.

"Emma, I know you hate me, but please just leave me alone." I looked into her cold eyes.

She grabbed my arm firmly. "Melody, come on, stop this now! It's two days a week when most people have to work five to six days a week, full time. You are going to help take the pressure off your dad. Show him you care."

Emma loosened her grip on my arm, and the tone of her voice softened. "And if you are really serious about this boyfriend of yours, then he will think a lot more of you if you are trying to do something with your life."

Joyce patted me on my back.

My breathing started to calm. Chewing my sore lips, I looked at them both in turn, attempting to seek any sincerity in their faces. Both of their heavily made-up faces had softened, but I felt far from relaxed in their company.

I slowly nodded my head.

"Great. You start on Saturday," Joyce said.

5
FRANK HOLTON
JANUARY 2017

Nate walked into my office, looking harassed.

"Frank, we have a guest who is not happy. Apparently, they booked a sea view. But our system says they have booked a standard room. Do I change it?" Nate asked.

"Do they have proof of booking a sea-view room? And do we have a sea-view room available?" I asked.

At that moment, Molly rushed in, huffing and puffing, nearly knocking Nate over.

"One of the guest's manky kids has thrown up in the dining room. It's everywhere, and it stinks. Every time I try to clean it, I nearly throw up too. And the bloody mother is complaining of the smell while she is trying to finish her dinner with her fancy man."

It never rains but pours! I made a quick decision. "Nate, go and help Molly with the vomit. Where are these sea-view-wanting guests? I'll see to them!"

"They are in the..."

More bloody interruptions! I held up my hand, gesturing for them all to be quiet as I answered the phone.

"Hello, Holton's Boutique Seaside Hotel. Frank speaking."

"Hey, Frank, it's Elly from The Soul Rhythm Sisters. I'm sorry to do this to you, but we're going to have to cancel tonight. All three of us had a dodgy takeaway last night and we are feeling rotten. We will refund you, obviously, and I hope you'll want to book us again. I'm so sorry, Frank."

I held my free hand over my forehead, closed my eyes tight, and breathed in deeply.

"OK, Elly. Listen, do you know anyone who can replace you last minute?"

"Erm, no, but we can rebook? I'm sure we will be better within a few days."

"That's good to hear, but we've nearly sold out all the tickets, and we have the hotel guests wanting to see you tonight."

There was no reply.

"I hope you all feel better soon." I put the phone down.

How the hell am I going to sort this out by tonight?

"Nate, where are the sea-view couple, and what's their name?" I asked again as I stood to leave the office.

"In reception, Mr and Mrs Green – and there is no evidence of them booking a view room."

"Thanks, Nate. Go and help Molly sort out the vomit mess, please." Nate and Molly turned to leave, but a couple that appeared to be in their early fifties were blocking their exit.

"Where is this manager? I'm sick of waiting around. I want to know what's going on?"

Nate turned around to face me. "The Greens," he mouthed, ushering them in as he and Molly left.

"Mr and Mrs Green, please come in. I'm sorry about all

this. I'm Frank Holton, the manager and owner of this hotel. Take a seat. I'm sure we can sort all of this out."

Mr and Mrs Green sat on the sofa opposite me.

"I understand there has been a confusion with your booking. We have you down for a standard room, but you say you have booked a sea view."

I checked the booking system to see if Nate had made a mistake, knowing that was highly unlikely.

"We booked a sea-view room! We should be settled in by now, starting our mini break, but instead we've been waiting for hours, having to deal with amateurs!"

Mrs Green continued to glare at me. The computer showed they'd checked in at 2.00 p.m., and had been waiting twenty minutes. I'd had many guests pull a fast one before. My late parents used to lecture me on this all the time and would deduct the missing earnings from my wages. They wouldn't speak to me for weeks, apart from providing me work instructions. Nothing came before their beloved hotel.

"Do you have a print-out of your booking or maybe an email of your booking on your phone? That'll settle this." I provided Mr and Mrs Green with my signature charming smile.

"Are you accusing us of lying, Mr Holton? You really are running a terrible hotel here!"

My forehead was throbbing, so I rubbed my temples.

The office door opened with a bang.

"Frank, the vomit has been cleaned up and Nate is disinfecting the area again. That stuck-up cow is saying her child's vomit has ruined her and her fancy-man's meal, and she wants a replacement for free. She didn't even help with her own child's mess!"

Molly slammed her fist into my door where there were

already numerous impressions and I was puzzled as to how she'd avoided breaking through the wood.

"Frankie! Honey!"

Oh, dear lord, this really was the last thing I needed.

Lilly pushed past Molly without a care in the world, her denim shorts exaggerating her toned hips, as she sashayed in and blew me a kiss with her full Botoxed lips.

"Are you blind, Lilly?"

Lilly didn't turn around to face Molly, but just rolled her eyes and sat on my desk, facing me. Her enormous breasts, barely covered by her crop top, were proudly on display.

"I'm going to have a field day on Tripadvisor." Mr and Mrs Green nodded to each other in agreement, and I was brought back to my depressing reality.

"Mr and Mrs Green, I'm so sorry, this never normally happens. Molly, would you please get our guests a free drink, and I will talk to *you* later."

I looked back at my computer, checking which rooms were available.

"We should not be giving them anything for free, Frank. We should be chucking them out of here!" Molly said, stamping her foot like an irate child.

"Dreadful behaviour." Mrs Green tutted.

"Excuse me, do you want to say that to my face, lady?" Molly approached Mr and Mrs Green.

"Molly, get out now!"

The throbbing in my head was beginning to affect my vision. I'd almost forgotten Lilly, when she said, "Honey, I need some money. Me and the girls want to go to Bea Lane Spa – they do the best facials in the world. Anyway, it's a need, not a want."

Lilly placed her manicured hand on my thigh, pushing her large bosom towards me, and pouted.

"Is this hotel also a brothel? You really do disgust me, Mr Holton."

I was awoken from my daze, disgusted with myself. I pushed Lilly away so she was sitting back on my desk. She frowned and pouted like she was about to start another tantrum. I stood abruptly but had to hold on to my desk for support, waiting for the dizziness to pass.

"Frank, I need this facial. You don't understand! Please, it's only five hundred pounds!"

"Five hundred pounds for a facial! What's in it? Liquid gold?"

I heard a muffled squeal followed by an explosion of laughter.

"That will do you wonders, Lilly," someone said. "Even better if you eat some of it."

I looked up. Aunt Bella was grinning. She'd smeared a slice of Victoria sandwich all over Lilly's shocked face.

"That is the best thing we have seen since we arrived here." Mr Green chuckled raucously, with Mrs Green joining in.

"I'm not going to stay here and be bullied like this. I'm leaving!" Lilly wiped the cake off her face and stomped out of the office.

Aunt Bella approached Mr and Mrs Green, stooping slightly to shake their hands. Wearing one of her long, flowered maxi dresses, she looked like she was attending a cocktail party. Mr and Mrs Green both returned her handshake, with a genuine friendliness I hadn't yet witnessed.

"I've been informed of everything, and I'm sincerely sorry to hear about all that has happened since your arrival. By way of apology, please allow us to offer your stay here – including breakfast and evening meal in a sea-view room – free of charge."

I nearly choked and sat back down in my chair.

Aunt Bella fished a room key out of her pocket, placed it in Mrs Green's hands, and then walked over to my desk, where she had a tote bag full of Tupperware boxes. She retrieved one of the boxes and handed it over to the couple.

"These are the best jam tarts you will ever taste – ask anyone in Whitebridge Sands. Book your evening meal at reception. Breakfast is between 6.00 a.m. and 10.00 a.m. We will ensure the rest of your stay with us will be wonderful. Oh yes, and before I forget, this evening's entertainment has changed – and for the better. Tonight, Fish, Chips, and Mushy Peas will be singing for us." Aunt Bella lifted the Greens' cases like they contained nothing.

Fish, Chips, and Mushy Peas...

"Follow me, dearies!"

"You could learn a lot from her. Who is she anyway? Does she work for you? We didn't catch her name?" Mrs Green asked.

"Bella Holton, my great-aunt. And yes, you're right, I am very lucky that she's happy to teach me." The Greens gave me a polite smile before following Bella.

Aunt Bella had always been more than just a great-aunt: she was the one who truly saw me, amid my parents' endless focus on the hotel. Her presence was a steady comfort, a warmth I hadn't often felt, especially since their passing. She was family in a way that truly mattered.

There was a selection of open Tupperware boxes laid out in front of me, filled with homemade sausage rolls, fresh honey-glazed ham sandwiches, and Aunt Bella's famous triple chocolate cake. My stomach rumbled, and I was drooling over the alluring aroma. I could no longer help myself and shoved as much food in my mouth as possible. I couldn't remember the last time I had eaten.

"You eat up, my boy. Plenty more where that came from." Aunt Bella sat back on the sofa, deep in reflection, twisting her wedding ring.

She looked up a minute later. "I know you're cross with me, Frank, but the hotel was going to get a terrible review, and maybe worse, after what happened today. A dramatic offer had to be made, even if they were telling porky pies."

"I know. I messed up big time today, and you really saved my ass again. But I've got this, Aunt Bella. I can make a success of this place." The tightness in my forehead had eased, and I could focus again with comfort.

"I know you can, son, but even your parents had breaks, and there were two of them – manager and assistant manager, you know. Jackie on reception has been worried about you for some time, and mouthy Molly had mentioned you weren't coping. Maybe…Jackie would make a fantastic assistant manager, and that would give you a break. You can't live your whole life here."

The rich, smooth chocolate melted in my mouth, and I grabbed another slice of cake from the Tupperware box. *Melody would love this.*

"I don't need the help. It's all fine here. Just an adjustment period, that's all. Anyway, are you sure about Fish, Chips, and Mushy Peas? I know you're supporting Margaret, but a singing group in their seventies and eighties…I don't know, it sounds like something that should be in a cheesy bar."

Aunt Bella shook her head.

"Frank, don't be so ageist! I informed as many ticket buyers as possible about the change of entertainment so they had the opportunity of a refund. For hotel guests, it's free anyway. And, for anyone that turns up, it will state on the board what type of entertainment it is tonight. So, stop ya faffing!"

It wasn't just about the hotel, though she'd undoubtedly saved it from a terrible review. Aunt Bella always had a way of cutting through the chaos, of seeing what I needed even when I couldn't. She worried about me, pushed me to take breaks, and reminded me there was a life outside the endless demands of the hotel – a life my own parents had tragically overlooked in their dedication.

Later, standing at the back of the hotel's moderately sized function room, I could oversee the whole event. At one end, there was a full bar with numerous multicoloured stools and glass tables, and at the other, a dance floor and small stage. Fish, Chips, and Mushy Peas – three elderly ladies – were dressed in vintage 1950s dresses, their grey hair done up in tight curls, and all three were wearing bright red lipstick. They were not the best singers in the world but, my god, they were entertaining this crowd.

Margaret, the main singer, was Aunt Bella's roommate and best friend. She flashed her spotty stockings beneath knee-length bloomers and coyly covered her mouth with a hand tipped in red nail polish. When Aunt Bella had first introduced me to Margaret a couple of years ago, she would barely give me eye contact, never mind go on stage and sing to a crowd. Margaret has often told me how grateful she is for Aunt Bella. The devotion to their friendship is evident every time I see them.

"I knew they wouldn't let you down, son." Aunt Bella brought me out of my thoughts.

"Are you their manager?" I chuckled.

"I suppose I am, in a way. Another string to my bow." Aunt Bella stood proud in a semi-tailored flowery green dress. Her long grey hair, which was decorated with a matching emerald flower, flowed down to her lower back.

The singers were all shaking their arthritic hips, wiggling their wrinkled fingers in front of their faces, singing the Beyoncé classic 'Single Ladies'. Children and adults in the audience were copying their movements, with everyone laughing out loud as the singers blew kisses to several of the men.

The song ended and the singers waved me over to them, greeting me with a toothy grin.

"Before we continue, we have a special announcement to make," Margaret said. "As some of you may know, Sally and Austin Holton, the previous owners of this hotel – Frank's parents – tragically died in a car accident just over a year ago today. Not only did Frank have to come to terms with a huge amount of grief, but his parents' wishes were for him to take over the hotel immediately if anything happened to them. So, Bella, the girls, and I want to congratulate you on how well you are doing with this beautiful hotel. Would you come up to the stage, please, Frank?"

The crowd applauded. I faked a smile to everyone who stared at me with admiration, and my heart sank to the pit of my stomach. Oh god, I didn't deserve this. My parents used to run this hotel like clockwork. I ran this hotel like a clock running on sticky-toffee pudding.

Aunt Bella nudged my arm, which brought me back to reality.

"Come on, son," Aunt Bella whispered as she put her arm through mine.

We arrived on the stage. Margaret guided us to a trolley

covered with a sparkling cloth. The ladies stood around it, holding a piece of the fabric each.

"Come on, everyone. Five, four, three, two, one!" The audience joined in, and the cover was removed.

I gasped. I really didn't deserve this. They were all pensioners; how had they afforded this?

"Bella told us that Frank has loved photography since he was a young boy, and we wanted to help make his dream come true with a camera set and professional photography course." The audience applauded, and all four looked at me with hopeful eyes.

This was not just a camera set: this was a Nikon professional digital camera with accessory bundle and an online course at the British Academy of Photography. This must have cost them well over two thousand pounds. I held on to my stomach, worried that Aunt Bella's triple chocolate cake would be revisiting me.

"What's the matter, son? Everyone's staring, let's go." Aunt Bella tugged on my arm.

I grabbed the microphone from the stand and look straight at the ladies.

"No, I'm sorry. Thank you so much, Aunt Bella – and Fish, Chips, and Mushy Peas – for my wonderful gifts. They're great, they really are. Ladies and gentlemen, please enjoy the rest of your evening."

Escaping into my office, I sat at my desk, leaned forward on my chair, put my hands on my stubbly face, and rested my head in my hands.

"You've been here all day. It's time for you to get some sleep."

I hadn't heard Aunt Bella come into the room.

"Aunt Bella, I'm sorry for earlier. I don't know what—"

"It's fine, son. I love you dearly."

My heart felt so much lighter than normal, no longer weighed down with heavy rocks of guilt.

At that moment, my office phone rang, and Aunt Bella answered immediately.

"Hello, who is that?" Aunt Bella said in a cheery tone. I rolled my eyes. We had discussed so many times how she should answer the phone.

"Oh, James! How are you? How are the girls? We've had a fabulous night this evening. You should all come down here."

While Aunt Bella continued the conversation, I tried to hear what James was saying.

"Yes of course you can. He is right here. Oh, James, do you remember when Frank and Melody were kids and they had that pretend wedding in my garden. Oh it was adorable!" I knelt next to Aunt Bella.

"Yes, Yes! And they gave everyone cups of dirt and worms for the wedding breakfast." Aunt Bella belly laughed.

"I'll pass you over, James. He's hovering next to me like an annoying fly." Aunt Bella passed me the phone.

"Frank, how are you? I'm sorry it's so late to call, but I really need to talk to you. I'm at my wits ends, and I don't know what to do with Melody anymore. Things are a nightmare here."

The throbbing in my forehead returned. I looked over at a photo of Melody and me on my computer screen and instantly started to worry about her. I was under the impression she was doing much better. Had she been lying to me all this time?

"Tell me everything, James. I want to help."

6

GRACE BRAXTON

JANUARY 2017

A ping on my phone informed me I'd received an Instagram message from Tina.

> Hi Grace,
> My Christmas was good and I couldn't face going back to teaching. I could have stayed in bed for weeks.
> That counsellor doesn't seem to have a clue. I've had similar experiences.
> You're not a burden. I'm happy you're here, and I'm sure your dad is too.
> Remind me what other treatments you've had.
> Do you follow 'Taylor The Teacher298'? I've been messaging her, but I've received no response. I would like to ask her advice on how she is managing so well in her career and life, when she states she has chronic pain. I get that I can work part-time, but as you know I'm unable to do anything for the rest of the week, and you are struggling to do anything at all.
> Lots of love, Tina xx

Why did Tina ask some of those questions? I wondered. They seemed a bit random. I was beginning to feel a little sleepy and tried to snuggle back down into my bed.

"Grace...are you awake?" Melody whispered close to my ear.

"Mm hm," I grunted.

I was in a warm cocoon of freshly washed bedding that had a lovely aroma of citrus fruits. I was reluctant to sit up because it had taken me so long to settle into a comfortable position that allowed me to sleep for a few hours. My body was usually in a blaze of fire, yet I must have found a comfy position as the heat had cooled.

"Please can we talk?" Melody placed her cold hands on my arm.

Forcing open my exhausted eyes and gritting my teeth, I said, "Hold on, Mel. Let me get myself awake."

My body reluctantly moved to my command, punishing me with extreme pain. I gradually adjusted myself into a sitting position while my sister sat twisting my office chair, staring at her phone. She appeared completely unaware of how painful my manoeuvre was.

"What's going on?" I asked.

Melody raised her head to look at me. By the dark, heavy bags under her eyes, it looked like she'd had less sleep than me.

"I've ended up with a weekend job at one of Joyce's stupid salons, and I start tomorrow. I'm really scared, Grace. I don't want to go, but Emma seems to think I need to start contributing to the family and that I'm causing problems for Dad. I asked Dad about it, and he thinks it's a good idea too. Can you believe it? Emma and Joyce were awful to me. More than usual. They were making out I'm this awful selfish person!"

Melody now paced up and down my room, continually running her hands through her frizzy hair.

"I know how horrible the Wicked Witch of the East Midlands and her minion can be...but this could be good for you, Mel..." I hesitated, holding my breath.

Melody immediately stopped pacing and directed her hurt eyes towards me.

I continued. "Wait, wait...I don't think that continuing to isolate yourself like you are doing is any good for you. And I think Dad could be really poorly, Mel. I think he should see a doctor." I shivered, attempting to pull the thick duvet towards me. Melody landed on the bed next to me, our fore-arms touching.

"What! What about me? I'm not isolating myself. I just like to be at home or help with Dad's business. What's so wrong with that?" she asked.

Melody folded her arms and knocked me accidentally. The bump caused an electrical spark of pain down my spine. I gripped the nearest pillow.

"There's nothing to be ashamed of if you're struggling with anxiety and depression, you know," I said to her. "We could look at getting you support."

"There is nothing wrong with me!"

"We need to look at the reality of the situation. This family is at crisis point."

Melody shot up from my bed like a firework, knocking off a few cushions on her way. Our relationship was important, yet my battery was on a daily rate of twenty percent, and she drained a huge percentage of that.

Melody stood poker straight, her lower lip trembling. "If you think the weekend salon job is so great, Grace, you take it!" she shouted, storming out of my bedroom and slamming the door behind her.

"You have no idea how much I would love to be able to do that. Any job, in fact," I whispered to my empty bedroom, closing my tired eyes.

∾

The ringing of my phone woke me from my nap.

A male voice asked, "Am I speaking to Miss Grace Braxton?"

"Yes, speaking?"

Trying hard to open my heavy eyelids, I reluctantly dragged myself into a sitting position, disturbing the comfy cocoon I'd been happily lying in. I needed to wake myself from my fatigued state.

"Miss Braxton, my name is Liam Davis, and I'm calling from Edford University. We received your CV regarding the Student Proofreading zero-hour position. We are very impressed by your CV, but we do have a few questions. Are you OK to speak at the moment?"

My heart leaped. "Oh yes, please go ahead."

"I can see you are highly educated with excellent grades. You were an assistant editor for a publishing house, and it looks like you were on your way to becoming an editor. We wondered why you wanted to apply for this role?"

"Sadly, due to a decline in my health, I had to leave my employment at the publishing house. However, I'm eager to keep working, especially to support others to reach their dreams, such as the students at your university."

I stretched to grab my A4 notepad and pen from my bedside cabinet.

"OK. Thank you. That explains the gap in your employment. Also, thank you for the information you provided for us in the separate letter and references. Both the role – and the necessary training – can be completed at home via our software. We will send you everything you need. Your manager would send you assignments, the deadlines, and how much you will be paid per assignment. From there you decide whether you would like to accept or decline. For the first month, your manager will review your proofreading to check everything is OK before submission. Does all that sound OK to you?"

"Yes, great, brilliant." I scribbled everything down. My eyes kept going in and out of focus, and I felt as though I could have easily fallen back into a deep slumber.

"Wonderful. Henry Bell will ring you in a few days to go through the next steps with you, and I will send you the information packs now via email."

"Great, thank you very much."

I felt the happiest I'd felt in ages. I was going to work again.

"You seem very happy, duckie, which is lovely to see," Zoey said, arranging my table for lunch.

Wearing a very bright pink-and-white striped wool jumper, Dad leaned over me. He placed a sandwich and a cartoon of juice on my bedside table.

"I've some wonderful news. I've got a job. Well, it's a student proofreader role – a zero-hour position. It's a good way for me to brush up my skills, and the gap in my employment won't look so bad. I can help more financially in the household, and I can do all the work from my laptop."

My developing smile disappeared when Zoey and Dad looked at each other with concerned expressions.

"I don't mean to be awful, duckie, but you struggle to do basic tasks. How are you going to cope with this job?"

Dad gently pushed a stray strand of hair behind my ear.

"I can do it all from my bed," I said. "I'll be fine. And I get to pick and choose my assignments. I need to make sure I have a career when I recover."

Zoey cleared her throat. "I admire your ambition, Grace, but you're pushing yourself too hard. I see how much daily life is exhausting for you. How about you read instead? I know you were saying how much you used to love to read. You deserve to have enjoyment in your life."

I looked down at my floral nightie. Zoey was wrong: I didn't deserve any enjoyment in life. How could I? I didn't work. I'd only allow myself enjoyment when I'd accomplished productivity and hard work.

"Anyway, we'll talk about this later," Dad said. "We have a surprise arranged for you. So, finish your lunch, and let's get you dressed, ready, and in the car as soon as possible." He playfully shoved Zoey, who laughed.

"Surprise, well, wow, this is so very kind of you both, but I don't..."

I took a deep breath. I didn't want to upset them, especially as they had gone to so much trouble, but I needed to get on with the preparation for my new job. I couldn't waste my energy on pleasurable experiences.

"No, come on, Grace, I know exactly what you're thinking. If you are not well enough, that is fine, but I'm taking your laptop and research books away as well so you can completely rest."

Dad sighed heavily, took a handkerchief from his jeans pocket, and wiped his forehead, which was perspiring heavily.

"I'm sorry, Dad. Yes, I'm very grateful. Thank you." My gut twisted.

"You're going to love this, duckie," Dad said as he left my bedroom.

Zoey supported me into Dad's car. Even with her kind assistance, I was exhausted. I was in the front passenger seat with my head back, trying to calm my throbbing muscles.

Dad was leaning on the driver's door, and he was inhaling and exhaling at a rapid rate.

"Dad, are you OK? Please sit down. Do you need a doctor?"

I was trying to push my body as close to him as possible, but each movement brought sparks of agony. Zoey brought my dad a bottle of water, and he plonked himself down on the driver's seat. His breathing started to calm, and I placed my skinny hand on his.

"I'm sorry, girls. It's been a long time since I've put the wheelchair in the boot, and it took my breath away. I obviously need to cut down on the pies." He chuckled while patting his belly.

"Don't worry, Mr Braxton, I'll get the wheelchair out when we get there." Zoey got into the back seat.

"Thank you, Zoey. By the way, Melody was involved in

planning this surprise for you, duckie. She wanted to make up for her bad behaviour the other day, but she is currently sulking in her car."

"I'm sorry, Dad. I think I added to that. I didn't mean to – it all came out wrong," I explained.

"No need to apologise. I just struggle to know what to do for the best for our Melody. Listen, I spoke to Frank the other day, and he's coming to visit us soon, but please don't tell Melody. Frank has a big opportunity for her and I don't want her to freak out."

"That sounds positive. I won't say anything."

"We're here!" Zoey said, bringing my attention to our destination. I couldn't believe my eyes when I saw a huge sign outside North Litten Library that said: 'Amber Levendale Author Talk & Signing – Tickets Only.'

"Have I told you lately what an amazing dad you are?"

"Go on, tell me. I told you, I knew you'd love this." Dad chuckled.

As we went into the library, Zoey asked, "How long have you been a fan of Amber's books, Grace?"

"I can answer that," Dad cut in. "Since she was a young girl. Grace has always been mature for her age, and her reading was always above those in her class. If she felt lost or sad, she read Amber's books. If she felt happy, she read Amber's books. You get the picture?"

Zoey brought my wheelchair to a stop. Dad presented me with Amber's new hardback book, *Guardian of the Stars – Strikes Back*. The glossy cover shone in colours of vibrant silver and mauve. I ran my fingers over the smooth texture, and joyful tears filled my eyes.

"Thank you so much." My huge smile made my cheeks ache.

"I need to nip to the bank, won't be long. Go on, duckie, you go and get it signed." Dad nodded at Zoey. My heart leaped in excitement as I spotted Amber surrounded by fans.

Zoey manoeuvred me between the shelves until we reached the back of the queue.

"I'm just going to get us a drink from the machine. Would you like a hot chocolate?" Zoey asked.

I nodded yes, and Zoey went off to get the drinks.

North Litten Library had always had a special place in my heart. Melody and I used to spend hours here, especially as children. The beauty of it was, we could be reading completely different books, but when we spoke about our latest literary adventure, it was like we were discussing our latest thrilling holiday. Maybe we could do that again one day if we ever got back to how we were.

"Grace Braxton. Oh dear! You really have gone downhill, haven't you?"

I was brought back to cruel reality by my ex-best friend, Josie. She was looking at me like I was a scab on her otherwise perfect skin. To my horror, I could see she was wearing a staff badge, showing she was working for one of the most famous publishing houses in the UK.

"Get out of that wheelchair, Grace. Give it to someone who really needs it."

She leaned forward and stared me down with evil eyes. She positioned her arm on my armrest in a way that caused my wheelchair to lean in her direction. My nails pressed into the armrest, my heart was pounding, and I let out a scream, thinking my chair would tip.

"Get away now!" Zoey demanded as she strode towards Josie. "People like you disgust me."

Josie jumped back, and my chair stabilised, bringing it back to centre. However, the jolt as my chair landed back on the floor shot pain straight up my spine. Everyone around us stared. Embarrassed, I kept my head down.

"What's just happened? Is everything OK?"

I raised my heavy head.

Wow, it was Joy Olivewood, the CEO of Dolphin Publishing. I couldn't believe I was in front of this actual legend, and I must have looked like a vulnerable mess. I sank further in my wheelchair.

"No, everything is not OK. I can see this *lady* is wearing a similar company badge to yours. She nearly had my friend out of her wheelchair." Zoey pointed to Josie, who looked like a rabbit caught in headlights.

"No, no, it was just a misunderstanding. Grace is an old friend. I bent down to hug her," Josie stuttered.

"Rubbish! You must be thick, or something, love. You're surrounded by a group of witnesses here," said a tall man who appeared to be in his twenties, holding his girlfriend's hand.

"And you weren't whispering when you were telling the lass in the wheelchair she was a faker!"

The girlfriend nodded, and the queue around us murmured in agreement.

"I'm sincerely sorry about this. I'm utterly shocked at this outrageous behaviour. I assure you—"

Josie interrupted by standing in front of Joy. She stood tall, smoothing down her tight office dress that barely fitted her frame.

"Mrs Olivewood, please don't talk about me like I'm not here. I've a right to have my side of the story heard as well."

The entire library went silent; you could have heard a pin drop.

"Josie, get out of my sight, and I will see you at 9.00 a.m. in my office tomorrow morning."

Josie marched out. She pushed over a stack of information leaflets, and as she reached the library doorway, she mouthed, "Pathetic Bitch."

"Free hot chocolates and biscuits for everyone!" a library assistant announced while filling two tables with refreshments. The fans crowded around the treats.

"I'm sincerely sorry, everyone, about the delay and the upsetting events. Amber will continue signing books shortly," Joy explained to the fans.

They moved me to the front of the queue with no protest from the other fans. Joy walked towards us as we sat at the table where Amber had until recently been signing her novels. Zoey sat next to me, sipping her hot chocolate. I was attempting to hold back the tears that kept trying to escape from my eyes. I should have been grateful to be there; I was going to see my favourite author. But I didn't deserve it. It had been so long since I completed a hard day's work, so I understood why Josie turned against me.

Zoey squeezed my hand gently and brought me back to the moment.

"Can we go home, please?" I said, wiping away a tear that had managed to get away.

"Can you manage another five minutes, Grace? I don't like the thought of you missing out on meeting Amber." Zoey's kind eyes begged me to stay.

And then my author hero approached us. "Hello, Grace, you won't miss out on our meeting. I apologise for keeping you waiting. I was starving – needed more than a few biscuits to keep me going."

Amber laughed as she elegantly sat down on the seat opposite me.

I was in awe. I couldn't help but stare at this wonderful lady. She was the reason for so many of my happiest reading moments. I could have kissed her marvellous brain!

"Sorry, I think Grace is a little star-struck. She has been a huge fan since she was a little girl," Zoey explained.

"Actually, Grace, I believe you and I have been in contact before. I thought I recognised you from your former staff photo when I saw you in the queue. Can I just check if your name is Grace Braxton?"

"Yes, that is correct..."

"I won't go into too much detail, but it was about six years ago, and I was going through a real rough time in my life, and to cap it all, my publisher and agent dropped me. I thought I'd lost everything, and my confidence in writing vanished. So, a friend suggested a way of getting back out there was writing under a pseudonym, and I managed to find a different agent. Anyway, my agent at the time got me with K & L Publishing House, and guess who my main point of contact was. Guess who it was that gave me so much support and the confidence I needed to kick some writing butt."

My heart felt as though it would burst with joy. I raised my palm to my chest.

"My pseudonym was Lucy Perkson. I wrote a few romance novels under that name. When I left the publishing house and got back to being me again and wrote my fantasy novels, I wanted to invite you to join the celebrations, but no one would tell me where you were. I imagine it was a confidentiality policy."

"No way! I'm always telling Grace she's amazing, but she never believes me," Zoey said.

"Amber, are you saying I was a part of your writing journey?" I asked.

"A part? Grace, you saved my writing. You saved me!" Amber came over to me and embraced me in a warm hug.

"Hun, could you get us all another drink?" Amber winked at Zoey, who left the table in search of more drinks. Amber sat back down.

"How are you feeling? I'm sorry about what happened with that awful cow. I only caught bits of what happened, but I will make sure she has nothing to do with me or my work again."

"I'm fine, I just want to get back to work. I can't stand being like this any longer." I raised my arms wide to display my wheelchair. "But sorry, yeah, I didn't mean to moan. Congratulations on your new book. I can't wait to read it."

"Have you read *Guardian of the Stars,* the first book in the series?

"Yes, I've read all of your novels."

"Do you remember how Juliet Locks was in her greatest battle, and her enemy nearly destroyed her planet and her people – and in the battle, she lost the cherished powers that she'd had since she was a child? Well, she felt of no use to herself or her tribe. She was close to sacrificing herself to the gods. Thank goodness, Juliet discovered just in time that her tribe loved her for who she was and not just for her powers—"

Amber's story was interrupted by my dad's approach. "There you are," he said. "Sorry I've been so long. I didn't think it would take all that time. The banks need to know everything these days. I'm surprised they didn't ask for my blood type."

His face dripped with sweat.

"Shall we get going, duckie? Looks like there are a lot of people wanting to see Amber."

Joy returned, tapping at her watch.

"Yes, we get the hint!" Amber rolled her eyes at Joy.

"It really was a pleasure seeing you, Grace. Thank you for everything."

Amber slid my copy of the book towards her, signed it, and slipped a card inside. Then, to my surprise, she held my left hand with both of hers. "I hope you enjoy my latest novel, and please reread *Guardian of the Stars*."

7
MELODY BRAXTON
FEBRUARY 2017

"You do know how to use a brush and pan, don't you, Melody?" Joyce clicked her fingers in front of my face.

The pungent smell of ammonia, chemicals, and a whiff of fragrant shampoo made me nauseous. I was surrounded by ear-piercing chatter from customers and staff talking about rubbish. Combined with the whoosh of the hairdryers, snipping of the scissors, and the constant ringing of the telephone, it was all too much.

How many people in North Litten possibly needed their hair done?

"Melody! Am I talking to myself? I'm not paying you to stand there. Sweep the hair with the brush, sweep the hair in the pan, then empty it into the bin!"

Trying harder to capture my attention, Joyce waved both her hands in front of my face.

"Now, Melody!" Joyce yelled, startling me into action.

"You'd think she would be grateful to you. Kids today have no idea what a hard day's work is," said a middle-aged woman with foils in her hair.

Joyce walked towards her, peeled back a piece of foil, and then smoothed it back down.

"You'll be ready in five minutes, Dalilah, and yes, I'm trying to give her some dignity. We all go down the wrong path from time to time, but it's about picking ourselves up, isn't it? We can't stay wallowing there forever and expect everyone around us to pick up the pieces all the time." Joyce turned around and raised one of her tinted eyebrows at me.

I hated her.

"You're such a good person, Joyce. You're giving her the skills she needs to look after herself," Dalilah said, continuing to browse through the pages of an old magazine.

I took the pan filled with hair and disposed of it outside. Then I moved away from the bins and paused to take in a deep breath of fresh air.

"Hey, New Girl," someone said, interrupting my attempts to calm my heart and mind. "Boss wants you to make a round of drinks. Four teas, three with milk – and two, add sugar, and two coffees, both with milk, and one wants sugar." The hairdresser, who looked like she'd barely left school, disappeared before I could ask where the kitchen was.

Luckily, the salon didn't have many rooms, so I managed to find the way easily. I searched through all the kitchen cupboards – and there were a lot of them; the kitchen was surprisingly large. Once I had the items I needed, I placed them in a row and waited for the spotless white kettle to boil. I twisted my new hair bobble tightly around my wrist, even though it was beginning to cut off the circulation.

Four teas, milk, sugar, two coffees, milk, and sugar. No, four teas, three have milk, and two have sugar. Two coffees with milk and one has sugar...

"Melody, they're hot drinks, not science projects!"

Joyce popped her horrid head around the door frame. I felt like my heart stopped for a moment, and my bobble snapped.

I spotted a tray across the room. The kettle clicked.

Four teas, with milk and sugar, but two coffees with milk and no sugar – or was it four coffees, milk, and sugar...?

My hands trembled as I poured the boiling water into the mugs. I had to use my other hand to attempt to steady the one that shook. Not surprisingly, some of the water missed the mugs.

With all the drinks ready, I quickly cleaned up the spillage. Then I balanced the heavy tray on my palms and fingertips, though my hands continued to shake. The walk towards Joyce and the other clucking hens felt like doomsday.

Every pore of my being wanted them to disappear. *Please make it stop!*

I sweated more each second, and I had no idea how my heart remained in my chest, as the beverages were starting to make a pool on the tray.

Joyce walked over to me and my jittering tray. Placing her hands on her hips, she said loudly, in front of everyone, "Look at this mess, and why are you just standing here? Why haven't you handed these drinks out?" She grabbed some paper towels from the reception desk.

"I don't know whose drink is whose," I mumbled.

Joyce held the bridge of her nose and closed her eyes for a second.

She took a spotty mug from the tray, wiped the bottom with the paper towel, and moved the mug towards her mouth. "I'm dying for a drink. This is mine, right? Tea, milk, no sugar?"

I could almost hear the static coming from my brain.

Instead of providing a coherent answer, I provided a staggered breath.

Joyce shook her head in frustration. She took a large gulp and then spat the contents over my face.

"That's vile."

I dropped the tray, and the mugs smashed into pieces, emptying their contents all over the floor.

"Melody!" Joyce threw me the paper towels.

I took a step forward, then slipped backwards in the puddle of caffeine. I landed with a wallop – luckily, not landing on too many broken pieces of pottery.

"I'm surprised she didn't break your floor, Joyce. I think the whole street moved when she landed." Dalilah exploded into laughter, with the entire salon joining in.

I jumped to my feet within seconds. Not caring about my appearance, I pushed open the glass double doors and ran out of the terrible place.

I ended up outside Patrick's office. An Edwardian property, surrounded by a large car park, with a moderate beer garden in the back, where he used to take me when he was working nights. I smoothed my frizzy hair back with my sweaty hands and walked into the reception. My heart lifted as I saw him standing there, speaking to someone at the desk.

"Patrick, do you have...?" He turned around and looked me up and down like I was a car that needed a drastic repair. His attention was taken by a pretty twenty-something receptionist.

"I'll be with you in five minutes, alright?"

I gasped at his response. It felt like a knife to the heart. He spoke to me like I was one of his friends down at the pub.

Speaking to the young receptionist, he said, "We'll just finish going over the booking system, but you know where my office is, sweetheart, if you need anything."

"Thank you, Mr Rutland." The receptionist bit her bottom lip.

"So, when you have completed the booking, you click confirm here." Patrick leaned over the desk and placed his hand over hers, which was hovering over the computer mouse.

"Will you click on my little mouse, Mr Rutland?" she said as they held intense eye contact.

"I'm such a fucking idiot!" I shouted out loud before running out of the building and slamming the doors behind me.

I stumbled down the street, seething. Hot tears blurred my vision, and I couldn't catch my breath.

I really can't cope anymore. I can't do this anymore. I just want this all to end.

The slam of a car door brought my attention to the moment, and the first thing I was aware of was Patrick's alluring scent of Old Spice and cigars. He grabbed the back of my hair and roughly pulled me towards him. His lips pushed aggressively onto mine, and for a few moments, I was taken to a pleasurable place that only he could take me.

Yet, my mind wouldn't let me forget the awful events that had happened only minutes earlier. I pushed him away, even though my heart desperately wanted to succumb.

"Leave me alone. Get back to your receptionist." I turned to walk away.

Patrick grabbed my forearm and dragged me towards him, his fingers digging into my flesh. He placed one of his large arms around my waist and cupped my chin with his free, strong hand. "Come on, Sexy Secretary. I was just helping a new starter. Don't get all jealous on me." He laughed.

"You do talk crap, Patrick. I bet you've shagged her already. You haven't replied to my messages. Just let go of me!" I attempted to squirm out of his stronghold.

"I've just been really busy, baby. Let me make it up to you, please." His grasp became tighter. He passionately kissed my neck and nibbled my ear. Despite myself, I was already melting into his arms.

"I need to get you in the car. Now, baby. I've got your second favourite treat in the car, and you can have it if you are a good girl," he whispered in my ear.

Patrick had parked his car down a quiet alleyway, and we'd had sex. As he'd zipped up his jeans, he'd passed me a small see-through bag containing my second favourite treat. And as though nothing had happened, he drove me home.

"That was fantastic. I'll call you later," he said as he kissed me quickly on the lips, and I got out of the car.

"Don't smoke it all at once," he said, laughing as he sped off.

I stuffed the small bag into my bra and walked up the cobbled drive, humming a happy tune to myself.

As soon as I walked into the house, Dad was there.

"There you are, Mel! We have been waiting for you. Blimey, what's happened to you?"

Dad looked in despair at my caffeine-stained leggings, my ruffled hair, and the sweat stains on the white shirt I'd been ordered to wear to the salon.

"Babycakes! I've missed you." Frank rushed up to me and gave me a warm hug.

"Come on, let me see you, fellow crazy cat lady," Aunt Bella called from the living room.

"Frank, let her go. We'll all go into the living room. Aunt Bella has brought some of her amazing cakes." Dad smiled at us both as Frank freed me from his arms.

"I don't mean to be rude, but were they smoking strong, damp cigars in the salon?" Frank said, wrinkling his nose.

Ignoring the comment, I followed Dad into the living room, with Frank in tow.

"Today really didn't go to plan. I'm surprised Emma isn't kicking off at me right now, but it's so great to see you guys!"

I went over to kiss Aunt Bella before sitting next to Frank on the sofa.

"Emma's at her swimming club. She'll be late – you know how serious they take it." Dad leaned back on the opposite sofa, close to Aunt Bella.

As I'd sat next to Frank, the sofa had sagged, making us bounce into each other. We kept bouncing into each other's shoulders, which made us both laugh hysterically.

"You two haven't changed since you were kids." Aunt Bella chuckled.

"Go on, everyone help yourself to my lemon tarts. I don't want to be taking them home. Get them eaten, please."

We all reached for the creamy, overfilled tarts.

"Tell us what happened today, then, duck," Dad said.

Milly jumped on the sofa next to me, purring. She placed her adorable head on my thigh, and I gently stroked her. Automatically, she gave me a sense of calm as I told my woeful story of the day, without mentioning Patrick.

Aunt Bella cooed at Milly from a distance.

"Well, actually, that does bring us to the reason why

Frank and Aunt Bella are here today," Dad said, turning his brown eyes to focus on me. "I will be honest with you, Melody. I'm very worried about you and your future. I've spoken to Frank, and we've come up with a really good plan. A brilliant opportunity, in fact, but it would have to be done at a slow pace."

I looked round to Frank, who patted my hand gently.

"What do you mean?"

My heart beat faster, and as my left leg tapped repeatedly on the floor, I startled Millie, who jumped down and ran to another room.

"The idea is that you move in with me. You have your own room – you know your own space. Then we would gradually give you hours at Aunt Bella's cat sanctuary. It would be a new start. You'd be doing your dream job, and we'd be able to spend more time together. We all think this would be great for you, babycakes." Frank tentatively smiled at me.

I was beyond furious. Standing up, I took one of the cushions from the sofa and hurled it across the room, screaming for added effect. It narrowly missed one of Emma's favourite ornaments. Dad, by this point, had his head in his hands.

"Stop that behaviour, sweetheart. We are trying to help you here. And think about all the cakes you can eat and all the adorable fur babies you can care for. It'll be marvellous!" Aunt Bella said.

Frank gently pulled on my arm. His warm touch brought comfort, but all I wanted to do was scream at my father.

"Dad, you said I could stay here forever. Why are you doing this to me? I bet Grace doesn't have to leave, does she? You always favoured her because she's more like Mum."

Dad rose out of his chair very slowly, sweat dripping from his face, appearing unsteady on his feet.

"Dad...please answer me," I begged.

Aunt Bella rushed to Dad's assistance.

"Melody, it's obvious your father is not feeling well. Sit yourself down."

Aunt Bella helped my dad out of the living room.

Frank got up from the sofa, walked across to me, and held me lovingly in his arms. Exhausted, I lay my head on his chest, and he gently stroked my hair. His steady heartbeat helped me to settle, and gradually my tears lessened.

"Melody, I really hope you are not turning down this opportunity because of Patrick and your love of weed? I'd hoped that chapter of your life was over. A better life is waiting for you, and you have people here who love you, willing to go above and beyond to help. Even your dad has taken a massive loan to pay for your living expenses while you get settled."

8

EMMA BRAXTON

FEBRUARY 2017

Walking into the living room, I couldn't believe the carnage before me. Thick pieces of sharp glass were left around the fireplace, and shards had fallen onto the cream carpet. Holding a bin bag in one hand, I knelt to collect the broken pieces of one of my biggest achievements. The glass was shattered so badly that the engravings were no longer visible.

I gasped on seeing how much crap Melody had left all over the place. Used underwear in bundles near the sofa, dirty cups on the table – and the games console was out again, with accessories left strewn in a long trail from the TV. I should have binned all her belongings when I had the chance.

"Ouch." I winced as I cut my finger on the sharp edge of the glass.

James staggered into the living room with his newspaper and collapsed onto the sofa. I stared into his eyes, hoping he would give me some comfort or explanation for this mess.

"What are you sucking your finger for?"

Annoyed, I gestured at the mess.

"Did you know my Swim England National Championship trophy for the four-hundred-metre individual medley is smashed into a million pieces?" I blinked back tears.

"Melody didn't handle her emotions well last night and ended up chucking her stuff all over. She let off some steam."

"That's acceptable, is it? Destroying my possessions?"

"Give over, Emma. You have got plenty more all over the bloody living room!"

I ground my teeth.

"More importantly, I don't know what we're going to do about Melody. I thought I had the answer with Frank's place, but she just freaked out about it. I've written to that hospital where Grace is on the waiting list, but they can't do anything about it, because we're waiting for the funding. I really don't know what to do next."

James ran his hand through his grey hair. I turned away in an attempt to control the volcano of fury threatening to erupt.

"Emma, are you listening to me?" He slammed his newspaper on the sofa.

"I'm fully aware of the situation, James. It's all we ever talk about!" I sneered.

"Do you know, Emma, all I can talk to you about is nothing!" he said, opening his paper aggressively.

Pain tightened my throat. I placed my hand to my gullet.

"I'm not allowed to be upset that my trophy, showing my biggest achievement in my professional swimming career, is broken? My house is trashed. My sister gives Melody a great job, but she causes havoc, yet you don't even have a go at her! Am I ever allowed to talk about myself or us, James? Ever?"

I stood quickly and glared at him.

Why was I never a priority? He promised me so much, and I gave up so much to be with him.

"Emma, I've seen such an evil side to you over the years. Think about other people's feelings, for a change."

"Do you mean I should be thinking about Psycho Lazy Arse and Insane Sack of Potatoes for every hour of my existence?"

I stared at my husband for several moments, but he wouldn't engage with me. He wouldn't even spare a second glance. He just got up and walked out of the room, slamming the door behind him.

～

I recognised the horrid smell. A pungent, earthy, musky odour – and it was filling the entire house. I walked to the end of the bungalow where the house connected to the garage. The adjoining door was slightly open, and the overpowering smell hit me in the face.

Melody's Nissan Micra was full of smoke.

I stormed over to the driver's side, opened the door with force, and found Melody lying back on her reclined seat, smoking.

"For fuck's sake, Melody! You are stinking my house out with your nasty drugs." I reached inside the car and snatched Melody's hand-rolled cannabis joint.

Melody laughed hysterically. Her flab jiggled, and tears of laughter were rolling down her face. I pressed the security key on the automatic garage door, and the heavy metal door opened.

"Let's show the whole street how pathetic you are. Seriously, how thick are you, Melody? Even if I'd gone out with your father as previously planned, we'd still have smelt this awful stuff like last time!" I threw the joint into a rain puddle.

Caressing the steering wheel, Melody said, "This steering wheel is so round. I love this steering wheel, Emma. Everything will be OK, Steering Wheel. Emma, where are the fudge brownies?" she asked, lifting her head.

I walked back over to the driver's side, leaned over, and peered into her dirty car. "I'm not going to let you, or your sister, treat me like a skivvy anymore," I said, grabbing hold of her fat face by her chin. I dug my long fingernails into her skin. "You two have been standing in the way of my happiness for far too long. You won't be my problem for much longer."

I shoved her back into her car seat.

"It's the only way to silence all the horrible things inside my head...I am sorry," Melody stuttered.

I turned to face her through the car window. A single tear dropped onto her pudgy cheeks. I stared for a few moments and wondered how I was going to deal with this whole situation.

I texted Joyce, suggesting we go out for the night.

9

MELODY BRAXTON

FEBRUARY 2017

"Oh my god!" Emma screamed.

I awoke abruptly from a deep sleep. I rubbed my hazy eyes, then wondered if what I'd just heard was a dream or reality.

"Melody!"

I heard Emma shout, "James, speak to me."

Without any further hesitation, I ran to Dad's bedroom.

When I turned the door handle, I couldn't open the door; there was a resistance like a heavy case on the other side.

"Don't push the door! Your dad's on the floor," Emma yelled.

"Emma, what's going on?"

My heart pounding, I placed my ear to the door.

I heard Emma shouting on the phone. "Ambulance, right now!"

"Melody! Please tell me what's going on," Grace yelled.

"Dad, what's wrong?" I asked through the door.

I tried to calm my breathing, but I was unable to stop the panic that was rising in my chest. I leaned against the door and slid down the wood to a sitting position as my breaths became erratic. Grace was shouting, along with Emma, who was demanding instructions from the paramedic on the phone.

"No. No. No! Please, not my dad."

"Melody! We don't have time for your tantrums today. Get away from the door. I need to try and open it for the paramedics."

I was about to stand when the door opened, and I fell over, surprised to see Emma looking down at me.

"Don't stress your dad out. I'm going to make a clear pathway for the paramedics, so please don't make a scene."

Emma pointedly wagged her fingernail at me, then made her way to the front door.

"Emma, Melody! Is Dad OK?" Grace yelled.

I squeezed between the door and the wall, went into Dad's bedroom, and looked behind the door.

"Dad!"

I tripped over my dad's right foot and fell back onto his bed.

I stared at him in disbelief.

This can't be real; this can't be happening.

"I am sorry, love, but we need to get your father to the hospital now." I flinched, not having noticed the paramedic's arrival. I reluctantly left the room.

Emma held me lightly by the shoulders. A tear dropped onto her natural skin. Without the usual makeup plastered across her face, she appeared much more human.

"OK, listen to me. Go and tell your sister that your dad is going to the hospital; there is no time to explain now. Then get in your car and drive to North Litten General. I'll meet you in A & E. I'm going in the ambulance."

When I'd told Grace how unwell Dad was, she'd asked me if I'd noticed how poorly he'd been getting. But, in all honesty, no. I hadn't. I'd only noticed he was slowing down – he was no spring chicken. My mind was like a carousel on overdrive; everything was going too fast. How was it possible for me to notice everything?

"Melody, the doctor wants to see us now." Emma broke into my thoughts.

"Come on through, Mrs Braxton. Hello, you must be Melody."

The doctor greeted us, then guided us through to a small side room.

I followed Emma into the room where we both sat opposite the doctor.

"Dr Buckingham, please just tell us how he is. The facts about my husband's health."

Emma took out a tissue from her designer handbag and dabbed her eyes.

"Mr Braxton has had a haemorrhagic stroke; he had an MRI…"

The room was going around in circles. I gripped the sides of my chair, trying not to fall to the floor. The overpowering odour of the antiseptic and chloroform made me nauseous. My clothes were beginning to stick to my skin, and I could feel my forehead sweating.

"As you are aware, Mrs Braxton, he is currently having emergency surgery, called a craniotomy."

He barely gave us the time to take this in before he continued.

"It's highly likely he will require specialist inpatient stroke rehabilitation, and we are unable to say how long he'll need for recovery time or how well he'll recover. The team helps patients to relearn numerous activities of daily living, such as speaking and walking."

A strong burning sensation pierced my throat. I doubled over and vomited – all over the floor, including on the doctor's shoes.

"I'm so sorry, Dr Buckingham. I will get you some new shoes," Emma said, evidently embarrassed by my actions.

With tissues from her bag, she tried to mop up the thick, potent mess.

Dr Buckingham asked, "Are you OK, Melody? How are you feeling now?"

I looked up to find the doctor at my side, his kind eyes studying me closely. I breathed a sigh of relief that the room was standing still once again.

"This should be about your dad, Melody, not about you," Emma said, retching as she continued the clean-up.

Dr Buckingham placed his hand on my arm and smiled at me.

"Everyone deals with traumatic news differently. It's nothing to be ashamed of. Don't worry about the rest of this. One of my colleagues will help. I will be back shortly."

"Would you be able to ask for an update on how my husband is? James Braxton," Emma asked the health assistant who'd come to clean the floor.

"Yeah, course," she said. "I believe you'll be directed to your husband's ward when they're ready."

When the health assistant and her trolley had gone, Emma stared out of the window. Taking a long, deep breath, she turned to look at me.

"I had a few plans to remove you and Grace from my life, well, not just my life. Mine and my husband's life. But I never went ahead with them, but now. Well, this has just made the decision very easy for me."

I shot up from my chair. "What! What are you talking about? Getting rid of us?"

"I never signed up to have you two in my life. Your dad told me that when we got married, he'd disown you both, but obviously that never happened. Your dad promised me so much, and I've wasted so many years. My good years!"

"Liar! Dad would never even suggest disowning us."

My heart ached.

Emma cackled. "There's a lot you don't know about your dad. Including how he made me abort your half-sibling."

I stood back in shock.

"No, Dad would never do that. And you can't chuck us out of our home. It's Dad's home as well, and he would never allow you to do that."

My thoughts were not able to catch up with my voice. It was like they were running after each other on a hamster wheel.

"It's my house, and I know you are a selfish cow, Melody, but are you really going to be that much of a bitch that you'll stress out your father. He's just had a stroke. We don't know what sort of state he'll be in after this operation, do we?" Emma smirked.

My entire body went cold. I stepped backwards, feeling for the chair. Lowering myself into it, I stared at her in disbelief. "I...I'll get the police, or some legal help or something." I shook my head frantically.

Emma cackled so vociferously that I wondered if the entire hospital heard.

"You are an adult who has been living in my house, who pays no rent or contributions. You have no right to live in my house. Stupid girl, you'll give the police a good laugh."

The door swung open, and a nurse said, "Mrs Braxton, Miss Braxton. James is out of surgery and now on the ward. The surgery was a success, but we do need to talk to you about what comes next. Will you follow me, please?"

"What a relief! Yes, please show us the way," Emma said as the nurse opened the door.

"Oh, thank god."

"I will mention before we get to the ward that your father, your husband, has been through so much today. Please be patient, and try not to overwhelm him. I imagine the consultant will only recommend a short visit today," the nurse said, closing the door behind us.

"We understand, don't we, Melody?" Emma raised her eyebrow.

The stomping of the feet, the chatter of the people, the judging of the eyes, and the beeps of the machine zoomed in on me.

I can't do this. I can't cope.

My vision was tunnelled on the exit, and everything else around me was out of focus.

I received two texts from Grace, one after the other, asking if Dad was OK. She'd texted me earlier, and I still hadn't answered. Nor had I answered Frank or Aunt Bella, who'd also contacted me for an update. The only text I'd sent since we'd been at the hospital was to Patrick, whose name appeared on the screen just as I was thinking about him.

He'd sent me his address.

I replied:

—I'm on my way, babe. xx

Entering the modern three-storey townhouse, I was greeted by my gorgeous man. Before I had a chance to speak, he pushed me against the hallway wall. He slowly nibbled my ear, kissed my neck eagerly, then aggressively pressed his lips against mine. A pleasurable hunger flooded through me as I breathed in the aroma of his cigar smoke. He moved his hands down my body, and I shivered.

I ran my hands through his soft hair as I sank further into the feelings of pleasure he elicited. My entire existence was filled with desire for him.

"Let me help you forget about everything for a while, baby. Let's go to bed."

Holding his hand, I followed his lead up a wooden staircase. I took a double-take as we reached the top of the stairs when I spotted a framed photograph wedged between a cactus plant and the opposing wall. The photo appeared to be of Patrick and a woman who looked vaguely familiar.

Patrick pulled me forward, then grasped my bottom with both of his hands.

"Come here, my sexy secretary. It has been a while since we have done it in a bed."

"Freshen up and let's go to the pub," Patrick said later. "Have a few drinks and get a pizza or something."

As he pulled up his worn denim jeans, I stared, admiring his beautiful body.

"Come on, beer supping time. I've left out a bar of soap for you and a towel."

I entered the elegantly decorated en-suite bathroom, which had tiles painted with gorgeous flowers. There were several small vases filled with floral potpourri, which all seemed very feminine for Patrick. I wondered if he'd recently moved and had not had time to change the previous owners' decorations.

Bar of soap and a towel. I laughed to myself. He'd been married twice before. You'd think he'd have a better knowledge of women. Lucky number three: maybe that'd be me. I took a deep breath and smiled.

Searching the bathroom cupboard, I found it full of products. Female and male perfumes, female and male deodorants, female and male shower gels, two used toothbrushes, and a packet of birth control pills prescribed for Miss A Turner.

My stomach lurched in repulsion, and I rushed to where I had seen the photograph on the landing.

"Baby, what are you doing!" Patrick shouted from the bedroom doorway.

I lifted the framed photograph to get a better look. To my horror, it was Patrick and that model from the market. In the photo, the model is hugging Patrick – *my* Patrick – and he has his arm around her perfect figure. They are gazing into each other's eyes like they are very much in love.

"You bastard!" I screamed, throwing the framed picture in Patrick's direction. The glass smashed around his feet, and he leaped out of the way.

"Jesus, Melody!"

I pushed past him and hurriedly dressed. Unable to stop my tears, I grabbed my belongings and sprinted down the stairs.

"I care about you," Patrick said, grabbing my arm as I reached for the front door. "I just find you hard to resist. You are my sexy secretary, after all."

I shook my head.

"I will never forget the day you and your dad did that house removal at Ma's place," he said. " You helped me after hours with all the paperwork. I can't tell you how grateful I am for that. Her death knocked me for six."

I turned to face him.

"Look, I am sorry," he went on, "but I never said we were back in a relationship again."

I tried to pull away. "You never wanted *me* to move in with you or anything more when *we* were together."

Tears streamed down my face as I gasped for breath. I felt like I'd been stabbed with a thousand knives.

"It's complicated, but *we* don't have to be complicated."

"Get away from me, Patrick. You're a monster!" I freed myself from his grip.

Patrick rolled his eyes.

"Just don't come around uninvited. I'll contact you."

"Fuck off, Patrick!"

10

GRACE BRAXTON

FEBRUARY 2017

I sent an Instagram message to Tina as I wanted to thank her for getting in touch.

Dear Tina,
Thank you so much for your phone calls. Especially last night, I was going out of my mind with worry. I got through to the hospital and my dad is stable after his operation, thank goodness. I'll ring again later to find out how he's feeling. Melody and Emma haven't responded to any of my messages or calls. In all the stress, I forgot to tell you that we received a letter back from the ambulance service about my dad's complaint. It's disgusting, they turned everything round saying we were the ones in the wrong, and out of a gesture of goodwill they won't take the matter further. Can you believe it? My manager has given me great feedback for my first proofreading assignment. However, I was penalised and marked down as I was two days late submitting it. I'm furious at myself for allowing this to happen

but will do all I can to ensure I do a better job. I cannot lose this job.

I don't know much about 'Taylor the Teacher298', I suppose we all experience chronic illness differently. Maybe some of her posts will give you an idea on how she manages her symptoms?

I hope you have a good day.

Love Grace xx

~

Zoey had come to help me shower while Mia prepared my lunch.

"There are two slices of bread and a tub of peanut butter," Mia said, appearing at my doorway. "The fridge and the cupboards are empty. I went to ask your sister, but she's conked out on the sofa and looks out for the count." Mia shrugged her shoulders and shoved her hands into her trouser pockets.

Zoey exhaled slowly.

"Peanut butter sandwich is fine, thanks," I said. Mia nodded and headed for the kitchen.

Zoey turned to me. "Look, Grace, I understand you're all going through an awful time with your dad and everything, but I'm really worried about you not eating properly. And this is not the first time."

I thought about this as she supported me into my pyjamas. "I'm sure Melody or Emma will grab me something, but thank you for thinking of me." I didn't look at Zoey; she'd know I was lying.

"I am not on again till tonight," she said, "but I'll bring you some snacks."

With Zoey's support, I reclined on my bed. My muscles

felt like they had been supporting a huge building, and relief washed over me as my entire body sank into the smooth mattress.

"Thank you. I really do appreciate everything you do for me." I smiled.

"You know this situation can't carry on like this forever, Grace. It's not good for any of you."

I heard her speak, but my eyes were already so heavy that I didn't have the energy to respond.

~

"Miss Braxton."

I attempted to unglue my eyelids.

"She is always sleeping, Sandra. I can't get her to stay awake," Emma said, dramatic tears creeping down her cheeks.

"Miss Braxton, it is important that I speak to you."

My eyes shot open, and pain rocketed through my spine.

"My name is Sandra Beldon. I am a social worker from North Litten Adult Social Services."

I slowly brought myself to a sitting position and reached for my support cushions and pillows. I breathed harshly as each movement I made sent a thunderbolt of pain through my body.

"I just can't cope! It's far too much, and you know, I now need to put all my energy into looking after my husband." Emma wiped away her crocodile tears with a dry tissue.

Sandra sat on my office chair and pulled numerous files from her bag.

"Go and get yourself a coffee – put your feet up. We will sort this, won't we, Grace?"

My stomach churned as Sandra winked at Emma, and Emma smirked at me as she left my room.

"The reason I am here today is because Emma has declared that she is no longer able to look after you, and from speaking to your father's specialist, with Emma's permission, it is highly likely that he will never be able to care for you again, either. It's more likely that your father will require care. Also, I've been collecting statements from your carers from the care agency and I feel you need more specialist care."

I began to feel sick.

"What do you mean *specialist care*?"

"That's what my team and I've been deciding. Emma informed me that you throw yourself on the floor, and North Litten Ambulance Service have provided me a statement with how many paramedic hours you've wasted with your behaviour."

"That is not true!" I said, and my body temperature soared.

"Your GP reports that your diagnosis does not fit your symptoms or this level of disability. He also thinks you are becoming addicted to painkillers."

I couldn't believe what I was hearing. "You need my permission to access my medical records, and I am an adult with full mental capacity. You should not be making plans for my care without my involvement! And my dad is only just recovering from a serious operation. He has not started rehab yet, so how is it even possible to know his full prognosis?" My eyes began to fill with tears, and I gripped my bedsheets with such intensity, my knuckles turned white.

"Please control your anger, Miss Braxton. I am only doing what is in the best interest for you and your family.

Don't lecture me about the rules and regulations, I've a senior role in the Care Quality Commission Board."

"You cannot remove me from my father's home, and I have carers coming in who take care of me." Warm, slow tears fell from my face.

"This house is purely in Emma's name, and she is no longer able to look after you – and is within her rights to have you relocated. The care agency also feel you are not receiving the right care at home."

I stared at her cold expression, too shocked to speak.

Melody stood in my doorway with Milly purring in her arms. "She's kicking us both out, Grace. She told me at the hospital yesterday that I have to move out." Looking as white as a ghost, she stared blankly at the floor as she spoke.

"As we don't have any suitable accommodation at present, as a team, we feel you need some in-depth assessments – especially your mental health – so we know where to accommodate you and how to meet your needs effectively. Therefore, either next week or the week after, you'll be moving into a nursing home. We're not sure how long for – waiting lists are so long these days. We will do your assessment there, and you'll receive care around the clock. They're specialised in behaviour problems. I'll leave you with all the information you need." Sandra placed several leaflets on my bed.

"Why are you doing this to me? Why are you punishing me for something I am unable to control? I am not *choosing* to live within four walls, being stuck in bed for the fun of it. It's because of severe pain." Now my tears were falling thick and fast. My entire body shook as if covered in freezing snow.

"Yes, I'm sure you're *really* in agony, Grace. So convincing..." Sandra laughed. Melody rushed to my side, sitting

Milly between us, endeavouring to soothe my tears by hugging me with her comforting, free arm. I looked down to my wrist and my butterfly tattoo, which always made me think of Mum. *If only I had half of her bravery, this wouldn't have happened.*

"Get out! You won't get away with this," Melody shouted.

"By the way, you can only take about two suitcases' worth of belongings with you. So, you will need to sort the rest of your stuff out rather quickly." Sandra scanned my belongings like they were covered in faeces.

I looked at my beloved books, my butterfly-themed collections, and my achievement certificates. The thought of reducing my entire life into two suitcases was too much to bear.

"Is everything alright, Sandra? I heard shouting." Emma stood in the doorway wearing a spa face mask and satin pyjamas, holding a glass of wine.

Sandra gathered her things and met Emma at the doorway with a smile.

"In a maximum of two weeks' time, you'll be able to concentrate fully on you and your husband. You've been through so much, Emma, it's time someone looked after you," Sandra said, touching Emma's forearm lightly.

"Our dad will never forgive you for this, Emma!" Melody shouted.

I curled up inside Melody's embrace, wishing – praying – that this was all a terrible nightmare. My body tensed, and pain flared. Milly's paws kneaded the bedsheets, the steady rhythm soothing me.

"If you have any problems with Shouty Sister over there, give me a call. I'm sure we can figure something out." Sandra winked at Emma.

"You're a miracle worker. Come on, let's celebrate over some wine. We've got that girl's weekend to plan," Emma said, and the two of them left my room.

"We're not going to let Emma win, are we, Grace? I bet you know what to do, don't you?"

"Mel, I think the Wicked Witch of the East Midlands has finally won."

11

MELODY BRAXTON

FEBRUARY 2017

The next day, Frank and Aunt Bella turned up to see us while Emma was out visiting Dad.

"Babycakes, sit down. You're going to wear the floor out," Frank said.

"Emma did what? You did what? You went where? I am totally lost," Aunt Bella said, slurping her tea.

I continued to pace up and down the living room, winding my hair tie around my wrist, more firmly with each twist. My heart pounded like a train racing along its tracks.

"Emma has even fixed it that Grace gets sent to an old people's home."

I paused, having done my best to bring Aunt Bella and Frank up to speed on what was happening.

"She told me to go to the Citizens Advice Bureau, the Jobcentre, the council – you know, those type of places," I went on. "I've had appointments with them all, and they were nice, but they couldn't help me with my problem. No one seems to understand. They kept trying to give me other advice, but none that was any good for me. And Grace said I can't tell Dad, because he is so poorly, which I get, but he's the only one who can help us. But Grace said we mustn't give him any stress because he is too unwell to handle anything. We have to let him believe everything is OK. But...but then Emma wins!" I took a gasped breath.

Frank stood up from the couch and placed his reassuringly large hands on my forearms. "Sit down with us. Let's talk this through."

He took my hand and guided me to the sofa.

"Have some double lemon sponge and tea, dearie. That'll help you feel better."

I slumped on the sofa and watched Aunt Bella eat a huge chunk of cake.

"I'm so confused, because what they've told me is I have no legal rights, and that's all they waffled on about. Legal stuff! So, I pretty much switched off to everything else they suggested, especially when they said I may have to stay in an emergency bed-and-breakfast housing thingy – and that's if there's availability. Then also I would have to fit the criteria and benefits. It was so stressful; I couldn't cope with it all. But they gave me all these leaflets and asked me to make another appointment if I need further help." I placed the leaflets on the table in front of Frank.

"Come on, Mel, have a piece of cake," Aunt Bella said.

She handed me a piece, which I popped into my mouth. It was delicious, one of Aunt Bella's best, but even tasting the wonderful zesty lemon buttercream, I couldn't fully enjoy it.

"I thought that would calm your thoughts for a minute or two," Aunt Bella said.

"Babycakes, I know you don't want to hear this, especially until your dad is back on his feet. You will either need to take up our offer – or I will see if I can help you make sense of these leaflets and appointments."

I swallowed the last of my cake and jumped up from the sofa, letting go of Frank's hand.

"No! I am sorry. I don't mean to sound ungrateful, but I can't leave here, I can't leave my safe place. I need to talk to Grace."

I ran to Grace's bedroom.

"I've done what you said, but it didn't work. They just went on about not having legal rights. You're the smart one. I bet you have more ideas." I landed on Grace's bed with a thump. Yet, the only response was Grace curling further into a tight ball.

"Grace, are you awake? This is important." I placed my hand on her cold arm.

"Be gentle, Melody. Your sister's in a lot of pain." Aunt Bella had followed me in and sat beside Grace. I winced with a pang of guilt.

"I can't believe what that evil witch has done to you both. Maybe we could get a bed downstairs, change the living room into a bedroom, and get one of those commodes. I think I still have my Jim's old one. Then Margaret and I could team together to do your care."

"Thank you for caring about me, Aunt Bella, but I could never put that on you. It would be too much," Grace whispered.

Aunt Bella stroked a piece of unkempt hair from Grace's pale face.

Frank cleared his throat. "If we can move Grace to your house, Aunt Bella, can we apply for care? Like how Grace has now?"

"We can enquire, can't we, Grace?" Aunt Bella suggested.

"I've got a feeling that awful social worker is going to make things very difficult for me, especially as she is part of the Care Quality Commission, though it doesn't stop us trying."

"Right, we need to do that now," Aunt Bella said.

"OK, I need to make some phone calls to the hotel, and I'll call the council as well." Frank left the room.

"Wait! Grace, what should we do next?" Melody demanded.

"Melody, don't you think it is obvious that your sister is suffering. You need to calm yourself down now, love." Aunt Bella gently waved an admonishing finger at me.

"I don't understand your problem, Melody. You've been provided a wonderful opportunity," Grace said quietly.

My chest suddenly tightened and I jumped up from Grace's bed. "You've no idea what it's like, Grace. You're so judgemental!" I shouted.

I stomped out into the corridor, slamming the door behind me, followed by Aunt Bella. She placed her hand on my shoulder, supporting me as we breathed in and out together.

"Let's leave your sister be for a bit, Mel, and let's start making arrangements for you moving over to us – while we eat more of my fabulous cake?"

"No!" I shouted, trying to make the demons in my head disappear. I pushed past Aunt Bella and ran into the adjoining garage.

I started my car then sent a text to Patrick.

—Meet me now! Or I will pay a visit to your precious girlfriend.

What do you want Melody?

—I'm on my way.

Fine, for fucks sake. I'll meet you at Ashfordby Lake car park. 10 Minutes.

The lake lay still and tranquil under a blanket of cold. The air itself seemed to hold a crisp, hushed reverence, as if nature itself had paused in silent contemplation. I heard crunching footsteps coming towards me.

"I'm guessing you haven't forcefully called me here for a quickie, then?"

"I need your help."

"I can provide you with sex and weed. That's your lot, babe."

"Do you not give a fuck about me at all?"

He let out an exasperated huff and threw his arms out. "What's happening? What is it?"

I explained everything.

"I'm sorry about your dad, but what do you want me to do about it all? That Frank and Bella have offered you everything on a plate. Go for it."

"I need to stay here!"

"What's here for you, really? Looks like your dad's going to need a lot of care when he comes out, and you don't really have anyone here. And obviously your dad's business will be gone. Start your life somewhere new. Look, I'll give you some money and weed to keep you going for now."

He handed me a wad of notes and an ounce of cannabis.

I accepted the items, but remained frozen. My heart seemed to shatter into countless fragments.

Patrick had never truly loved me. How many times did I need proof of this? He strode towards his car and drove off without even casting a backward glance.

12

GRACE BRAXTON

MARCH 2017

"I know. I can't believe it!"

My mobile was on loudspeaker as I was talking to Tina. I placed my phone on the bed and laid my head on the pillow.

"It is just perfect timing. I could come visit you as well. I don't live far from St Donovan's," she said.

A huge smile spread across my face. "Yes, I would love that. I better do something about my wreck of hair, though," I said, laughing.

"Don't worry about that. It'll be fantastic to see you, and I bet you will make loads of friends. You must introduce me to them, as well."

"You're a social butterfly, you are!"

"Don't be jealous. My focus will be on you," Tina teased.

Was I overthinking or was that a little strange? How keen she was to meet my fellow chronic illness friends and acquaintances?

"So, the funding is sorted as well? Everything is done and dusted?" Tina asked.

"Yes, my confirmation letter states I'll have a three-month admission to the Psychological Medicine Inpatient Unit at St Donovan's Hospital. The North Litten Clinical Commissioning Group confirmed full funding, and I'll be admitted the day I would have been taken to that hellhole."

"I am so pleased for you! It is a bit weird that it's a psychological unit, though, isn't it?"

"Yes, I spoke to my neurologist about this. He said not to let the name put me off – it's a multidisciplinary treatment approach to conditions like mine. It's going to be hard work, but I'll give it everything I've got."

"I know you will."

"I received the funding and the hospital bed a lot quicker than expected. I'm not sure why."

Aunt Bella suddenly appeared in my room and popped the cork of a non-alcoholic champagne.

As she poured the content into the glasses, she said, "Your dad and I bugged that hospital – and the money people – every day prior to him being admitted to hospital. I think they were planning to get a restraining order on me if I didn't stop sending them cakes and singing down the phone."

Margaret burst in with an operatic rendition of "Please give Grace Braxton the funding!" waving her arms in the air theatrically.

"That's one way to get your case heard," Tina said, and we both laughed.

"I better go now, Tina. But I'll speak to you later," I said, ending the call.

"Let's get this celebration started," Aunt Bella announced.

Frank and Melody walked into the bedroom, carrying one of Aunt Bella's homemade creamy carrot cakes. They both greeted me with a kiss on the cheek and Frank started playing uplifting music on his phone.

I smiled at Aunt Bella, who was wearing a long-sleeved cat-themed dress, which swished side to side as she sashayed to the music. Frank cut the cake, and Melody was quick to take a slice.

With a second slice in her mouth, Melody gestured for the others to help themselves to cake and bubbly.

"I would like to propose a toast to Grace's hospital admission and future recovery, to Melody's new career and life with us, and to James, who survived his operation and is starting rehabilitation," Aunt Bella announced.

We all raised our glasses in celebration.

"Did you get to speak to Dad today?" Melody asked.

I struggled to look her in the eye, her resentment hard to ignore.

"I spoke to the rehab ward. He has been severely affected by the stroke, but the specialist multidisciplinary team at the unit hope that – with hard work – they'll be able to bring some function back. The medical professionals looking after Dad have been great and are allowing me to have phone call updates, due to my circumstances."

I went on to tell them I'd spoken to Dad the night before, and my heart sank as I had difficulties understanding what he was saying. I could hear the heartache in his voice. I wanted him to tell me everything would be OK, but I held back my tears. It was *my* turn to tell him that everything would be OK.

Melody looked down and Frank put his arm around her.

Aunt Bella sat next to me. "You have always been so caring, and I'm so pleased for you, Grace. I was so worried about you going in that nursing home. I'm glad the hospital is doing the right thing. You're far too young to go in there. I mean, blimey, I'm far too young to go in there!"

The warmth of her hand on mine soothed me, and I wanted to reach out to her and hug her tightly, but the pain was too severe for me to sit up.

"Are the suitcases and bags for the hospital? And the boxes to go in storage, Grace?" Frank asked.

He looked at Melody. "Let's pack your stuff, too, baby-cakes. Once we've finished with Grace's." He turned to me. "Grace, you let us know what goes where. Stay as comfortable as possible." He stroked Melody's arm, and she gave him a half-smile.

"Yeah, I know. Well, I can always come back when Dad is recovered," Melody mumbled, trying to pull the hair ties off her wrist.

"By the way, Grace, we'll keep the stuff you can't take to the hospital and have your post directed to mine, then review everything after you are discharged, yeah?" Frank said, smiling broadly at me.

"Thank you, Frank." I took a deep breath. "I truly hope with all my being I will be back to my old self when I am discharged."

I lifted myself into a more upright position in the bed. Pain shot up my spine. I shut my eyes tight, clenching my teeth as I waited for it to pass.

"Apparently a cat's purr can help people cope with illness. Even if that is not true, you still get a nice warm cuddle."

Aunt Bella placed Milly gently on my lap. Exhausted, I opened my eyes and saw Milly curling up on my legs, purring away. I smiled inwardly, gently stroking the cat's soft black fur.

"Let's get this packing party started!" Aunt Bella attempted to juggle three rolls of masking tape, circus-style, but they fell on her head. We all exploded with laughter.

"Look at this photo, Grace. I found it at the back of the bookcase. Doesn't that look like a younger Emma in the background?" Melody handed me the photo.

I smiled at our happy family photograph, placing my finger across those who were no longer with us, and I felt a pang of loss for Aunt Bella.

"Look at the top, on the hill." Melody pointed.

I saw a hazy woman who looked like Emma. She was glaring at us and baring her teeth. A chill went down my spine.

"We didn't know the Wicked Witch of the East Midlands back then? Did we? We look far too young in the photo. Mum was still alive then," I said.

"Yes, I suppose you're right, but that's a spitting image of Emma. I'll go and show Frank. He must have taken the photo. He's been on the phone for ages to the hotel, he must be finished by now," Melody said.

Aunt Bella swiped the photo from Melody's hands and shoved it in her bra. "Come on now, ladies. We have work to do."

"Give it back, Aunt Bella!" Melody said.

Their wrangling was interrupted by Zoey, who entered my bedroom with a McDonald's takeaway. "Hello, everyone. I'm here for Grace's teatime call."

"Hello, dearie. Nice to finally meet you. I've heard a lot about you. I'm Bella, but most people call me Aunt Bella. Melody, let's go and have a cuppa in the living room." Aunt Bella shook Zoey's hand.

"Likewise. Nice to meet you, Aunt Bella."

"Aunt Bella – the photo," I called.

But she ignored my request as she and Melody left my bedroom.

Zoey brought my bed table across. "I heard your exciting news and thought I'd bring you a treat to celebrate." She placed the McDonald's on the table.

With all the excitement, fatigue washed over me. I was struggling to find the strength to eat or to even communicate.

"Thank you for always being so kind to me. I'll miss you, Zoey."

"I'll miss you too. It'll be strange not seeing you on a regular basis. Grace, where will you go when you leave the hospital?" She sat beside me.

"I've read lots of testimonies from people who've been to the hospital, you know, completed the admittance, and a lot have been able to go back to work. So, I'll be able to get my own place again. I've also been talking to someone online for a long time now. I really like her, and she said she's going to visit me in hospital."

"You've kept that quiet. Remember, Grace, you're worth your weight in gold, so you make sure she treats you like a princess."

"Thank you, I will. I know you've done so much for me already, but I'd like to ask you one more favour," I said.

"Yes, of course."

"Could you send these letters by Special Delivery for me, please? I've emailed these people as well, but in my opinion, a letter seems to get noticed more – and one of the recipients isn't great with emails. I've enclosed twenty pounds, which I hope will cover the costs."

I reached for the money and letters I'd hidden under my covers and handed them over to Zoey.

"Yes, I'll do it. First thing tomorrow. I must go to my next call, but I really do wish you all the best. Please look after yourself."

Zoey stood up, gently hugged me, and a small tear fell onto my cheek.

13
FRANK HOLTON
MARCH 2017

"Are you sure you're able to handle it, Jackie? Sounds like a rowdy lot you've got there," I said, rubbing my temples.

"We've got this under control. You don't need to worry. I'll ensure our good guests have a peaceful night's sleep, even if it means kicking the rowdy guests out," Jackie said.

"Dear lord, it sounds like we're back at school again. Please call me if you can't manage. I mean it, Jackie; I'll be straight over." I took a deep breath.

"Yes, of course I will, Frank. Go and enjoy your day."

Jackie ended the phone call.

Melody was crushing my hand. She'd barely let go since we'd arrived. There were still boxes and suitcases stacked in my car. Milly was sitting on top of one of my cabinets, surveying her new environment. The cat wasn't the only one who looked like she'd been caught in headlights.

I kissed Melody on top of her head, inhaling her beautiful floral aroma as I did so. Her whole body was quivering. Wrapping my arms around her, I hoped to calm her down. My heart ached. My babycakes had always been quiet; kept to herself. But somehow in the last few years she'd completely lost her sparkle. The sparkle that made her so special.

"I am determined to bring you back, babycakes. I want to make you happy," I whispered, and she squeezed me tighter.

I remembered her natural kindness, the way she used to light up when talking about cats, and her quiet empathy that often went unnoticed. That was the Melody I loved, and I longed to see her shine again.

"What's going on here, then? Why are all these boxes here? Whose are they?" Lilly stood in front of us with her arms folded over her large cleavage, leaving little to the imagination.

I tensed my fists. Oh god, I could have done without Lilly's drama.

I signalled for Melody to remain sitting on the sofa as I stood up to speak to Lilly.

"Lilly, I'd like you to meet Melody. Melody, this is Lilly," I said, looking at the volcano that was about to explode.

"Melody! THE Melody! Is she moving in with that dirty rat up there?" she said, pointing at Milly. Then she prodded my chest with her long fake nails.

"Lilly, please calm down. I was going to call you later to tell you everything."

"Tell me everything now! You really are a bastard, Frank Holton. You've never asked *me* to move in." Tears sprang to her eyes and her perfect makeup started to smudge.

The front door swung open and Aunt Bella burst into the room, wearing a bright pink ball gown. I couldn't help but smile.

"Hello, dearies. Are we ready for tea and cake?" Aunt Bella sang.

"You know I don't eat carbs, gluten, or sugar. Bella, please be more thoughtful – plus we're having a serious domestic here."

"I wasn't talking to you, and please wear more clothes, dear. I do find it rather disturbing. I have no wish to see your fuzzy area." Aunt Bella wrinkled her nose while looking at Lilly's ridiculously short skirt. Melody and I attempted to restrain our giggles.

Aunt Bella walked over to Melody and guided her by the hand to the front door, while Lilly continued to shoot evil looks at them both.

Lilly spun on her high heels back towards me. Placing her hands on her hips, she said, "Are you going to let that wrinkly pink toilet roll doll speak to me like that? This situation is far from over! Do you understand me, Frank Holton?" She wiped away her remaining tears.

"Lilly, I'll call you later," I said.

Her chin trembled. She pushed past Aunt Bella and Melody and marched out of my home.

As we guided Melody into Aunt Bella's vast garden, Aunt Bella covered Melody's eyes with her hands.

"I've been wanting to show you this for a very long time, my dear," Aunt Bella said, removing her hands.

What I saw made my heart jump with joy.

"This is the first time I've seen you properly smile in a long time, babycakes."

"Aunt Bella! This is incredible. I knew you looked after

cats in need, but this!" Melody looked around the garden again. "This is like what I pictured in my—"

Aunt Bella rubbed Melody's shoulders.

"Would you like to say hello to Mrs Mittens? She loves company, but no loud noises on those fancy phones. She's an old girl and likes her quiet," Aunt Bella said.

"Oh, yes please. I've read a lot about elderly cats' needs, especially with Milly getting older." Melody's smile stretched from ear to ear.

Aunt Bella led Melody to the sanctuary and unlocked Mrs Mittens' room. Melody entered quietly, sat on the floor, and after a while, Mrs Mittens gradually came down from her bed. The short-haired black cat rubbed against Melody's hand before settling onto her lap. The cat gazed up at me and Aunt Bella with pure joy.

Leaving Melody in her happy place, Aunt Bella walked back over to me.

"Speaking of a proper smile, son. What about yours? I know you love being with Melody, but I haven't seen your full-on beautiful smile in a long time."

"I'm fine. Just so busy with everything." It was a lie, and I could actually feel a headache coming on.

"Have you been using that fancy camera we got you? You need time for what makes you happy, son," Aunt Bella said.

A pang of guilt hit my stomach because I'd not even taken the camera out of its box recently.

"I will soon. It's just my photography's not on the top of my list at the moment. I've got too much to do." Then I quickly added, "But I'm still grateful for the gift."

"Life's not as long as you think it is, son." Aunt Bella tilted her head to make stronger eye contact with me. My body tensed. *What does she mean by that?*

"Frank! Aunt Bella! Mrs Mittens has gone back to her

bed. Can I have a look around, please?" Melody ran towards us with a big smile.

"You'll show Melody around won't you, son, while I get our tea ready?"

I nodded.

Aunt Bella stared longingly at her wedding ring.

Melody grabbed my hand.

"Frank! Look at all these beautiful cats," she said after she'd pulled me into the sanctuary. "It's like they have their own apartments, with their wrought-iron beds with colourful pillows. And look at the cat trees and how cute the white kitty is, playing with his mouse toy." Melody clasped her hands to her heart.

Her genuine wonder and the pure joy radiating from her as she saw the cats was infectious. It was this compassion, this pure heart that made her so uniquely beautiful to me, a side of her the world rarely saw.

"Aunt Bella and late Uncle Jim built this from the ground up. Your dream is Aunt Bella's reality. Jim made sure Aunt Bella's dream became a reality for her. He knew how hard she'd always worked."

Melody calmed her excitement down and I could almost see the cogs turning in her head.

"They've done a brilliant job. I'd never do anything great like this. I'd end up making things worse."

I sighed heavily. "We all have to work for our dreams, babycakes; they don't just happen."

Melody gave me a faint smile. To cheer her up, I tickled her under her arm. She tried to do the same to me, but I moved away too fast. I grabbed her again, holding her close, tickling her.

"I'll beat you up if you don't quit," she said. We both burst out laughing just a little too loud.

"Please keep it down. The cats don't like the noise," a volunteer said, frowning.

"Don't worry, Jake. I'll remove these naughty children." Aunt Bella winked at us both.

∾

"Don't be shy, dearies. Dig into the tea and cakes," Aunt Bella said.

The array of homemade cakes looked delicious – all moist, and the aroma of vanilla and chocolate was mouth-watering. I knew Melody was feeling the same, and she looked over to me for reassurances that she could dig in. I gave her a smile.

Margaret poured the tea.

"Hi, Margaret," Melody said with her mouth full. She swallowed her last piece of cake. "I like your T-shirt, Margaret. Is that your favourite meal?" She gestured to the logo showing fish, chips, and mushy peas emblazoned across her chest.

"That's the name of Margaret's band. Frank did all the brilliant photography for the website. Margaret looks like a rock star in those photos," Aunt Bella said, and Margaret beamed.

I could hear my phone ringing on the counter. My pulse quickened, and I rose from my chair without thinking.

"Sorry, ladies, that must be the hotel." I rushed over to the counter in the kitchen where Aunt Bella had made us place our phones. She never allowed *fancy phones* at the dinner table.

I picked up my phone and was hovering over the green answer symbol when Melody's mobile caught my attention.

Ten messages from Patrick Rutland.

Five missed calls from Patrick Rutland.

I slammed my fist on the counter. I knew that creep was back in her life after that day I went to see her at James's house, and she had that wretched smell of weed and cigars. She never answered me when I'd confronted her.

"It might not be what you think, son, and remember you are seeing Miss No Knickers."

I jumped to see Aunt Bella suddenly standing beside me, looking at Melody's phone.

"We need to go. Thank you for today." I hugged Aunt Bella, who was less cuddly than normal.

I took a mental note to phone her tomorrow.

"OK, yeah, I'll sort it out tomorrow. Thanks, Jackie." I finished the phone call and started my car.

"We've got an early start tomorrow," I said.

"*We*?" Melody asked.

I took a deep breath and squeezed the steering wheel.

"Yes, *we*. It'll be a gradual introduction, but we'll introduce you, give you a guided tour, then work out a work schedule for you," I said.

"But I'm not ready! I need to have a few more days, maybe a few weeks or so. Just so I can get my bearings and settle in," Melody said, a screech in her voice.

I squeezed the steering wheel harder to the point where my knuckles went white.

"Melody, I understand this is difficult for you, but you're coming across as ungrateful. Aunt Bella and I are doing everything we can to help you, and you are being a selfish, spoilt brat!"

Melody's eyes widened.

"I thought you were different, Frank, but you're just like everyone else. I needed to stay in my safe place. You know I can't cope."

Melody's left leg tapped repeatedly on the car floor as I pulled in to park at my house.

"I know your dad wants you to get on with your life and grow up! You have always had that selfish, immature part of you, but it was a small part in the background. Now it's becoming all of you. Even I'm starting to not recognise you." I got out of the car and slammed the door.

Melody opened the passenger door with tears streaming down her face. Anger boiled within me, but my heart ached when I saw my babycakes so upset.

"Give me the keys. I don't even want to look at you," Melody yelled.

The pain froze my heart, and I hurled the keys at her. They hit her chest before clattering on the concrete path. Melody's eyes widened. Picking up the keys, she sprinted to the front door.

"Go on. Ring Patrick. Let him break your heart again while you don't give a fuck about those who actually love you," I shouted.

Melody slammed the front door.

My head was pounding as I leaned over my car, tightening my fists and grinding my teeth. I stood, reached for my phone in my jeans pocket, and made a call.

"Lilly, can I come over?"

14

GRACE BRAXTON

APRIL 2017

My head rested on my hand as I lay on my side on the uncomfortable hospital bed, having a phone conversation with Aunt Bella.

"I've been here for more than two weeks now. It's been quite a lot to take in. They welcomed me warmly, but as soon as I got to my room, I broke down in tears. I felt so alone. Every day, there are visiting hours, and I see other patients getting visitors, but I stay isolated."

Aunt Bella stayed quiet, letting me get it all off my chest.

"For these past two weeks," I went on, "I've been living like I did at home, but with some help from the staff. They said they needed to do that to assess my situation. Soon, I'll have my first meeting with the team to talk about my recovery plan."

"Oh, Gracey, I am so sorry I am not there to visit you. As soon as I can, I'll be there for you."

"No, I am sorry, Aunt Bella. Your calls, cards, and gifts are most appreciated. I'm just moaning."

"Moan away, dearie. I want you to talk to me. Let the steam out of the kettle."

"I got a written warning from my boss. I'm so ashamed of myself. How am I supposed to get back to my career with this kind of performance? I've been missing deadlines. They even cut my pay, and I lost my Personal Independence Payment because I'm in the hospital. I have to go through another assessment when I'm discharged. I barely have enough money from Universal Credit to pay for my bills and basic needs."

I took a deep breath. "Maybe I can leave these financial worries behind," I said. "I've just got to get better. Work hard, take any job I can find at first, and then try and get back to editing."

"You are being far too hard on yourself. You can't possibly manage any employment while you are in so much pain."

I gripped the phone tighter.

"You need to concentrate on you. See how you get on with your pennies. I won't see you going without what you need. I'll send you some prunes to keep you regular too."

"Thank you, Aunt Bella. You are very kind to me." I smiled.

"And how is your dad, dearie?"

"Well, one of the nurses told me about his rehab plan. They're working on his speech, his movement, and his flexibility. I didn't understand everything, but it sounds like they're doing their best to help him."

"Good, good."

"But I feel so guilty when I talk to him on the phone. He gets frustrated when I can't understand him. And he keeps asking why we haven't visited. He says Emma's so nice to him, which makes me angry. I told him I'm too sick, and Melody moved in with Frank after thinking about his suggestion. But all he did was sigh."

"You're doing the best you can in a very difficult situation. James loves you girls; he will see the light."

We ended the phone call.

Aunt Bella always made me feel better. I then noticed I had a new Instagram message from Tina, and my mood lifted further.

I am back home, sorry again for not visiting sooner, but it was lovely seeing my grandparents. I can't wait to see you soon.

I replied:

—I look forward to seeing you and hearing about your time with your grandparents.

I also had a text message from Melody.

Grace, I found out that Dad seems to be doing better. Can I tell him what's going on yet? I am not doing well over here.

And I responded with:

—Thanks for asking about me, Melody. No, he has a long recovery to go.

"We take a holistic approach here. You will receive physiotherapy, occupational therapy, cognitive behaviour therapy (CBT), and we would also like you to engage in the social side – such as the groups – when you feel ready. We know from research that the combined methods of treatments can be very effective," Dr Herbert explained.

"Thank you. I appreciate what you're doing for me. But my biggest issue is the chronic pain. I can't engage in any of the therapies or the activities properly without better pain relief," I said.

"We are reluctant to increase your pain relief. The other methods will help with your symptoms over time."

"Dr Herbert, how am I even going to engage in the other methods when I am in so much pain that I feel faint and sick...?" I asked.

Dr Herbert turned to the other professionals in the room.

Still sitting uncomfortably in my wheelchair, the pain shooting up my spine, I looked at the circle of hospital staff. My entire body tensed as I recognised that, sadly, I had another battle on my hands.

Dr Herbert finished his conversation with the medical professionals and turned to look at me with a toothy grin.

"I want you to have your say, Grace, and this should be a shared decision-making process. We have taken on board what you have said. We will increase the dihydrocodeine to eighty milligrams, so two forty-milligram tablets up to three times a day. As I can see, you were taking the maximum dose of your previous prescription. Let's hope this will help with your pain relief."

"Thank you. I am grateful for that. Can I ask how the groups and CBT will help me with my recovery and my main goals?" I asked.

"People who have conditions like yours are prone to unhelpful thinking patterns and low self-esteem. We feel it's good to have that side of things addressed, and the groups provide a good outlet for you to meet others on the ward and support your mental well-being. Plus you may even learn new skills," he said.

Or you think my symptoms are psychological. I swallowed the bubbling anger. Did they all think a bit of therapy and some well-being groups would cure me?

"Grace, I understand your main goal is to get back to work and be independent again. That is possible if you put one hundred percent into this programme. We have great success rates, but only if the patients put in the work," Nurse Miguel said, waggling his finger at me.

I stared at the nurse blankly. "I am putting one hundred and ten percent into this."

Did he think I'd been at home playing computer games?

"Hello, Grace, may I come in?" A petite young girl was hanging onto my door handle with one hand and using her other hand to balance against the wall. She appeared to be struggling as the door was unsteady.

"Please come in. Have a seat."

Unsteadily, she walked to the armchair across from my hospital bed and landed on the chair with a thump.

"I've been wanting to say hello since you arrived," she said. "But I didn't want to overwhelm you. I know it can be daunting here. I saw you had some post, so I asked the receptionist if it was OK if I could bring it to you. A good excuse to introduce myself." She took my post out of her pocket.

"That is lovely of you. I must admit, I have been quite lonely, but I've not been able to join in with the others yet. What's your name, by the way?" I asked.

"Oh yes! What am I like? My name's Rebecca. You have a friend on the ward now. I'm in the room opposite you."

I smiled warmly at Rebecca.

"I love the beautiful postcards." Rebecca pointed at the large, carpeted pinboard that was just above my bed.

"My Aunt Bella sent me all those postcards, apart from the one from my sister and Frank. Aunt Bella runs a cat sanctuary for elderly, disabled, or unwanted cats. She and Frank take photos of the cats and turn them into postcards – a good fundraiser, as it goes." My heart suddenly felt heavy with how much I missed Milly.

"Your Aunt Bella sounds amazing! I love cats. I really do miss mine, but I was moved to a council property – a very inappropriate flat for my needs, and no pets allowed." Rebecca looked to the floor.

I tried to swing my legs off the bed and reach out to her, but a sharp pain shot through them.

"Oh, I'm really sorry to hear that," I said while trying to settle my legs back down.

Rebecca lifted her head and smiled brightly, wiping a tear from her cheek. "By the way, I get it about what you were saying earlier. It took me a month before I could join in with groups and mealtimes. And I can still only join the dining room for one meal, and I can't attend all the groups – it's too much for me. But I do feel I've improved compared to when I was first admitted. I hope that gives you some hope," Rebecca said.

"Yes, it does, thank you. I'm desperate to get back to my career – be independent again. It's unbearable to think of my life like this forever." I sighed.

Rebecca nodded. "One thing I'm starting to learn, especially when you have a chronic condition, is that sometimes we have to adjust our dreams, goals, and even our personal relationships if they have become toxic for our health."

There is no chance I am giving up my dreams or goals, I thought. *I am not living like this for the rest of my life.*

A loud knock on the door distracted our attention. The door swung open with a bang.

"Grace! It's so wonderful to finally meet you in person."

Time stood still.

I recognised Tina from her profile photo, but that was nothing compared to her beauty in real life. Her long dark hair cascaded over her shoulders like a waterfall and her curves sat perfectly.

I wanted to speak but was lost for words. I pulled the thin sheet towards me, trying to cover my body. I attempted to put my unkempt hair behind my ear, but my arms collapsed in exhaustion as Tina squeezed me. Breathing in her sweet scent of strawberries and vanilla, I shut my eyes briefly to savour the moment.

"How lovely to see you. I didn't know you were visiting today."

Rebecca got up and dropped the letters on my bed. "It was great to meet you properly today, Grace. Speak to you more later."

Tina gently let go of my body and turned around.

I smiled. "Yes, sorry, nice to meet you, Rebecca. Thank you for bringing my letter."

Tina cleared her throat. "Rebecca, hi. Can I ask what you were admitted for?"

"Tina...wow, that's very forward," I said.

Rebecca blinked slowly. "Oh, I have severe ME, and nothing seems to help. You know, medically. Anyway, see you later."

"Sorry, Rebecca. Yes, see you around," Tina said. She sat on my bed.

Rebecca struggled to walk out of the room. She grabbed on to every surface for support. I watched her with concern, wishing I could help.

"Grace, you look even more beautiful than your profile photo." Tina held my hand. My heart thrummed.

"OK, now I know my Aunt Bella must have sent you a cheque. I was thinking the same about you. But look at you, anyone who has eyes can see your beauty."

Our eyes locked, conveying a silent understanding that surpassed words. As if drawn by an invisible force, Tina's hand tenderly cupped my cheek. The space between us seemed to evaporate, and with a gentle yet deliberate move-ment, Tina closed the distance. Our lips met in a fervent dance, a collision of passion and longing that sent a shiver down my spine. The kiss started as a delicate exploration, a tentative brush of lips, then it deepened, becoming more heated and fervent.

"Is everything OK here?"

The physiotherapist's voice startled us. Tina and I jumped and broke our romantic embrace. I'd no idea he'd entered the room.

"Yes, everything is OK, Brett. Thank you." I tried to hide my smile.

"It's time for physiotherapy, Grace. You need to ask your friend to leave."

Tina winked. "I'll see you tomorrow and bring some chocolates and movies," she said, heading out of the room.

My cheeks flushed hot red.

Brett then left too, saying, "I'll be back in a couple of minutes."

I took the opportunity to read the letter Rebecca had brought me.

Dear Miss Braxton,

Thank you for writing to me, and I am sorry to hear about your situation. It sounds like the correct professionals and services are involved in your care. Therefore, I do not feel it would be appropriate for me to intervene.

I wish you all the best.

Yours sincerely,

Grant Franklin MP North Litten

I lay my head back on my pillow with a thud.

15
BELLA HOLTON
APRIL 2017

"You look a bit peaky, Bella. Are you OK?" Margaret asked while she dried the dishes next to me.

"Peaky! I look fabulous." I twirled in my strapless silk gown, paired with pink fluffy marigolds.

Pete smiled. "Another one of your beautiful dresses, Bella. Very nice, but I must say, I am thrilled to see you, Margaret. You look stunning as usual." He reached out for Margaret's hand and kissed it.

"Don't you two start a porno in this kitchen. Do it somewhere else, in private," I remarked.

"Sounds like we better get to your house then, Pete." Margaret winked. They both giggled like teenagers and held each other's hands.

"Can you hold on for maybe twenty minutes or so?" Margaret asked, gesturing at the dishes.

"Go on, I'll finish here." I waved them away.

I returned to the industrial-sized sink, continued to wash the dishes, and smiled warmly at my friend.

"You are good to me, Bella. See you later," Margaret said as she and Pete headed out.

I looked through the window to the clear cold sky.

"I'll never be with another man, my love. You'll always be in my heart," I said to myself out loud. I kissed my golden wedding ring. My heart still ached, like it did the day he passed away.

A loud, girlish laugh caught my attention. I refocused my awareness to the noise on the street. I saw Lilly with Mrs Holloway's grandson. Lilly just appeared to be talking, but she stood incredibly close, thrusting her breasts out, like a peacock.

Mrs Holloway was known for providing large donations to the community centre. The Holloways were practically royalty in our circle, and I doubted she'd like to see Lilly with her grandson. Mrs No Knickers was probably just attention seeking as usual.

"You're too wonderful to not find love again, Bella." I jumped back into reality to see Charles in his 'End Loneliness for All' charity T-shirt. The charity for which we all volunteered.

"Thank you, Charles, but I'm very lucky to have experienced true love. Is everything nearly finished for this morning?" I asked.

"Yes, everything's finished, but let me help you with the dishes." Charles reached for the tea towel and smiled, showing all his false teeth.

"I'm an eligible bachelor, you know. Plenty of ladies at this coffee morning want a piece of Charles. I own my own motor, my own flat, and I have a two-for-one National Trust membership card." Pete waved the tea towel in the air with enthusiasm.

I held my hand to my mouth, yet the explosion of laughter still managed to escape.

"Bella, can I spend the afternoon with you before my

show tonight?" I spun around and saw Margaret standing in the doorway, looking at the floor.

"Blimey, that was quick! What's going on, dearie?" I asked.

"We didn't even get through the front door before he got a *better offer*. I thought he liked me. I'm such a fool, falling for this rubbish at my age." Margaret's voice broke.

"Let me guess, Pete the Cheater? You're not a fool, love. He is a serial player. Definitely not a gentleman," Charles explained.

"What an awful man! I had no idea he was like that. Yes, of course Margaret. I'll just finish here, and I'll be with you."

"There's no answer. Maybe we should come back later?" Margaret tugged on my arm.

"I haven't got time for that." I took out Frank's spare key from my handbag and unlocked the door.

"Isn't that key for emergencies?" Margaret asked.

"Melody! Frank! Are you in?" I shouted, entering the house.

I started to look around.

"It's only us. We've brought you some goodies," Margaret said, cowering behind me.

I entered the living room and spotted Melody. She was sitting in front of the sofa on the floor, sobbing. She hugged her knees, stretching her large T-shirt over them. Strands of hair fell down over her face, tangled and unkempt.

"Come on now. Let's get you off the floor," I said when I reached her side.

Margaret helped me guide Melody up onto the sofa. Her

movements were slow as she eased herself back into her comforting position.

"Tell us, dearie, why are you so upset?" I placed a blanket over Melody's shivering body.

"Frank hates me! He thinks I am selfish and an awful person. And, well...that I've turned into a monster." Her voice was broken by gasps between her sobs. I rubbed her back gently, and Margaret squeezed her hand from the other side.

"Frank could never hate you, my dear. He thinks the world of you," Margaret said.

"I think he's stressed out, dearie. He's trying to balance so many things while trying to help you – and when you don't help, well, it can be very frustrating," I explained.

Melody looked up at me. "I don't want to hurt you, Frank, or anyone," she said. "Or be ungrateful for anything. But my mind is filled with dark clouds that block my clarity of thought. Sometimes I get flashes of fear and worry that make me panic. But other times I see a ray of hope shining through the clouds, and I chase after it with all my attention, thinking it'll make everything better and it'll end the hurt in my head."

My heart sank as Melody continued to cry. I hadn't realised she was struggling so much. Margaret and I made brief eye contact.

"Is that *hope* about going back home? Or about Patrick?" I asked.

"Both. I feel safe at home, and Patrick sometimes makes the circus of horrors in my head stop – even though he can be the cause of them too."

Margaret passed Melody several tissues from her handbag.

"Have you told Frank any of this, dearie?" I went over to

the bag of goodies we'd brought. I took out three wrapped slices of my homemade lemon drizzle cake. The lemon aroma made my stomach grumble.

"No," Melody whispered.

"I think that would be a good start. It would help him understand more; he can't read your mind," I explained with a smile. I passed the slices of cake to Melody and Margaret.

I was pleased when Melody began eating her cake with gusto.

"I don't want to cause you further upset, dearie, but from what I understand about your father's situation, the stroke has severely affected him. It may take him a long time to recover, and he may need further help when he's discharged," I explained as Melody shoved the last of the cake in her mouth.

"How about you reconsider our offer to work at the sanctuary? You can earn some pocket money and send your dad something nice; let him know you're thinking of him. I won't push you in to the deep end. We've drawn up a plan to make it as easy for you as possible, and it will show Frank you're trying," I suggested.

Melody's eyes widened.

"I'll try." She chewed her lips.

"I know not all of us are related, but I see all of you as my family. I have for a very long time. You, Grace, James, Frank, Margaret, and me."

We all smiled at each other in agreement.

"How's your sister, Melody?" Margaret asked, licking off the lemon cream from her cake.

Melody twisted her hair bobbles and looked at the floor.

"I don't really know. I've messaged her, but only asking when we can tell Dad the truth about, you know, what Emma did to us..." Melody explained.

A wave of nausea washed over me, and I placed my slice of cake on the coffee table.

"I'm concerned about Gracey, and I hope the treatment works as they said. Margaret and I are trying to find a place near us, but it's not easy, because we don't know how much assistance she'll need when she leaves the hospital. But I promise you, she won't end up in a nursing home," I said.

"Thank you for being so kind to us, Aunt Bella. Our mother was a nasty drunk, and Emma is the definition of an evil stepmother. I've no idea why Grace misses Mum so much, but we both feel like you are the closest thing to a mother." Melody wrapped her arms around me, and I felt a surge of warmth.

Was this what motherhood felt like?

16

MELODY BRAXTON

APRIL 2017

"Hi, Melody. We are having our monthly night out on Saturday. Do you fancy coming? All volunteers and paid staff are invited," Lauren said, giving me even more paperwork to complete.

"Sorry, I can't, but thanks anyway."

"OK, no problem. So, how are you fitting in? It's been a few weeks now, hasn't it?" Lauren smiled.

"Yeah, fine, thanks." I continued with my paperwork, hoping she would leave me alone. I never thought there would be so much admin for a cat sanctuary.

"Right. Anyway, good luck on your first night-watch shift tomorrow night. Don't worry, it's not heavy going. You look at the CCTV screens in the staff room, check everything is OK, see to the unwell cats if needed, and report anything that's wrong," Lauren said. "Oh, and make sure you turn off the gas stove, et cetera, when you're done cooking your tea. The room doesn't have much air circulation."

With that, she left the room.

My legs were tapping furiously under the desk, and I could feel panic rising at the thought of being alone in the dark with the possibility of having to make quick decisions. I really hadn't wanted to agree to all of this, but things were still not back to normal with Frank.

Although Frank was a great help to me, as always. He was supporting me with a plan to gradually increase my hours and expose me to the sanctuary and the community. To my surprise, this did actually help me cope with what might otherwise have been an overwhelming experience.

But, truth be told, the main thing keeping me going was knowing I'd be back home with Dad one day soon, and I would rejoin Patrick.

The shrill ring of the sanctuary phone was torture to my ears, causing me to snap one of the hair bobbles on my wrist. Out of the corner of my eye, I saw Frank walk in, and I quickly picked up the phone.

"Hello, Melody speaking. Can I help you?" The nervous twitch of my legs felt as though I was going to drill a hole through the floor.

"Melody? It's Grace. Are you OK?"

I sighed with relief, hearing Grace's voice.

"Yes. Is Dad out of the hospital?" I asked.

"No. Same as what I told you yesterday. Can I speak to Frank? I can't reach him at the hotel or on his mobile."

"Oh. Yeah, OK." I passed the phone to Frank. By now, he was standing next to my desk, and he forced a smile as he took the phone from me.

My heart ached as I looked at the framed photo on the desk of a much younger Frank, Grace, and me cuddled up on the beach together. We used to all be so close to each other – the best of friends.

"Melody, have a ten-minute break. Go get yourself a cuppa," Lauren said, snapping me out of my thoughts.

"OK." I smiled at Lauren and went outside.

Shivering in the chilly air, I wrapped my oversized cardigan around me.

My mobile phone vibrated in my pocket. I gasped with excitement when I saw who was calling.

"Hello, my sexy secretary. Guess where I'm going tomorrow night?"

"Where?"

"Whitebridge Sands. It's been far too long, babe. I need to see you. All this texting is not enough for us. We need to be physical."

The memories of our sexual encounters brought back a pleasurable quiver.

"I am desperate to see you. It would be great to make up, especially after how things ended when we last saw each other, but I'm working tomorrow and there is no one to cover me," I said.

"Work it out, babe. I will be with you at 6.00 p.m. tomorrow."

Patrick finished the call.

I walked back and forth down the garden path. What was I going to do? I needed to see Patrick. We'd made a connection again. He'd made all the effort to get back in touch with me – he wanted me back in his life, and I had to make sure he wanted me more than her! But at the same time, Frank would be furious with me, and I didn't want to hurt him.

"Time's up, Melody. Come on," Lauren shouted from the doorway as my stomach continued to churn.

Frank sat beside me at the desk. He placed his calming

hand on mine. I searched his eyes and wondered what he was thinking.

"I'm really proud of you, babycakes. I know this has been a huge challenge." Frank handed me a gift, and my heart lifted.

I unwrapped the gift within seconds, and when I saw what was inside, I gasped. It was a stunning digital painting of Milly, set in a paw-print-themed frame. Every detail of Milly's beautiful face, expertly drawn.

"I don't know what to say. Thank you so much. It's wonderful!" I continued to stare at the painting. Frank squeezed my hand.

"On Monday, we are all going to the hospital to see your sister and take her to see a specialist, Dr Evelyn Pinewood. Grace paid a lot of money to see her a while ago, and an appointment has finally come through. She needs our support, and we're all going to be there for her. You, me, and Aunt Bella," Frank explained.

"OK, yeah."

"Everyone here at the sanctuary is great, but having your expertise has been hugely appreciated, giving Aunt Bella some much-needed time to relax," Frank said.

"You really think I've been helpful? I am not really an expert," I said.

"You are – one hundred percent! Aunt Bella knew you would be."

A flutter of pride lightened the feeling that had been growing in my stomach.

Frank's expression then changed. He looked directly at me. "By the way, have you asked Grace how she's getting on in hospital? She says you haven't..."

"We've been concentrating on our dad," I snapped.

"You could ask Grace how she is. She's going through a lot." Frank's eyes tightened.

I ground my teeth. "She is being looked after in hospital, has support round the clock...doesn't have to go to work or face life. I am sure she is perfectly fine."

"Apart from the fact that she is in severe pain and is practically bed-bound. You know, the reason she is in hospital!"

Frank snatched his hand away and shook his head.

"I really shouldn't be here. Maybe we should go back to your car for a bit and then I'll get back to work, babe?" I stood up from the bar stool.

Patrick spanked my backside with such a hard slap that it knocked me slightly forward, making me grab the sticky counter to keep my balance.

"Sit down, naughty girl. We will get to that soon. I need my beer – I am parched."

I shrank back onto the uncomfortable chair.

The pub was heaving. Most tables were full of older men ogling the busty singer or reading newspapers. The overpowering aroma of sweat, cheap aftershave, and ale was nauseating. Over the years, we'd been to many pubs like this one back in North Litten, and I'd hated every one of them. When we were in a serious relationship, I'd asked if we could go somewhere different, but he acted like I'd offended his great ancestors.

"Come here, my sexy secretary. I've missed you." Patrick grabbed my hair from behind my head, pulled me towards him, and we embraced.

Eventually pulling away from him, I asked, "Babe, what

are we now? I mean, I know you're with her, but where do I stand?" I held my breath, waiting for his answer.

"You know, whatever happens, we'll always be best friends. Best friends forever." Patrick drained the rest of his pint.

My heart sank. I stared at the worse for wear, carpeted floor and wished I could sink into it.

Patrick lifted my chin, moved my hair to the side, and expertly started to bite my neck. I closed my eyes.

"Let me show you how much you mean to me. Finish your wine and get that sexy ass in my car."

I swigged down the cheap wine and followed Patrick to the car park.

"Oh my god! Oh my god! What's happened?" I placed my hands over my mouth. My heart was thumping like a jackhammer as I witnessed the event unfolding in front of me.

I swung back to where Patrick had dropped me off, but saw his car speeding away up the road.

"Where the hell have you been?" Frank yelled.

"We were worried sick about you, Melody. We thought you were trapped in the fire. My boy went in there, risking his life to find you, only to realise you'd gone AWOL!"

Aunt Bella glared at me, her lined face streaked with smoky tears.

I couldn't process what I was seeing. The whole thing played out in slow motion. Firemen moved in and out of the sanctuary, assessing the damage while two vets attended to the terrified cats.

Frank clapped his hands in front of my face, and I jolted

awake from the scene. He sniffed my hair, turned his nose up with disgust, and placed his hand inside my trouser pocket.

"Son, what in the world are you doing?" Aunt Bella asked.

Frank held up a small, clear bag of cannabis in front of me. His eyes were narrow with anger.

"You smell of that bastard as well," Frank spat.

"Please tell me you didn't leave the sanctuary to see that Patrick and smoke drugs, Melody? Not after everything we have done for you." Aunt Bella's voice broke.

"I am truly so sorry." I shook with tears.

"I can't even look at you, Melody. Please don't bother coming home tonight." A single tear ran down his face.

Aunt Bella clutched at her chest.

"Aunt Bella!" I cried. Frank and I hurried to her side, supporting her with our arms.

Her legs buckled as she lost consciousness.

17

GRACE BRAXTON

APRIL 2017

"I am exhausted after that," Rebecca said, wiping sweat from her forehead.

"You deserve these, ladies. Well done on your physio today." Brett handed each of us a cup of tea.

"Thank you," I said.

I massaged both of my legs, which helped to ease the pain that throbbed through them.

Back at my room, Rebecca looked at my pin board and started reading some of the notes.

"What's that blue Post-it note about?"

"Oh, before my dad became ill, he took me to see Amber Levendale. She signed her new book for me and left me a note with her contact details. The Post-it's just a reminder to thank her. She also asked me to reread the first book in her series – she thinks it will help me. Turns out I was her editor years ago, back when she was writing under a different name."

"How lovely. She sounds like a nice person," Rebecca said. "I love your cat stories, by the way. They really bring the photos of the cats to life." She smiled as she pointed to them.

"Thank you. I've been sending them to Aunt Bella. She says they've boosted their social media engagement. It's the first time in a while that I've felt useful." I hesitated. "But I'm so worried about her. She fainted recently and was sent to hospital. The doctors wanted to admit her, but she was not having any of it."

Rebecca was rubbing her hands, staring into the distance.

"Rebecca, are you OK?"

"Sorry, Grace. I do hope your Aunt Bella's OK."

"Is something on your mind? You don't seem yourself today, or is it purely the exhaustion of the physio, which I get." I smiled.

"I'm worried. The ward said they would help me with my living situation, but they're having difficulties. I used to live in a lovely bungalow with my boyfriend, but as my illness got worse, he traded me in for a healthier model." She looked at the floor.

"Oh, Rebecca, I am so sorry to hear this."

"It was awful – to be heartbroken, then chucked out of his house and placed in a high-rise council flat. I'm barely able to leave the place because I can't manage the stairs. The lift rarely works. And I can't order online grocery shopping because they won't bring it up the stairs."

"It sounds like a prison, but at least there you'd get three meals a day."

"You're right." Rebecca looked up at me with a tear in her eye, and I gently touched her arm.

"I am guessing you have no family to support you?" I asked.

"No. Like you, it's a complicated situation."

"I wish my mum was still here. She'd be able to sort out our situations with no problem. She was a hard-hitting journalist who took no crap."

"I'm sorry your mother's no longer with us. Sounds like we could've used her expertise."

"My sister and dad don't like talking about her; her name leaves a bad taste in their mouths. She did have an alcohol problem, but she was under a lot of pressure."

"Can't be easy for you."

"It's so wonderful to see you, Gracey. I've really missed you." Aunt Bella embraced me, her lavender scent instantly soothing.

"I've been really worried since I heard you were in hospital," I said, my voice breaking as I spoke.

Aunt Bella released me from her hug and sat beside me on my hospital bed. She rubbed my arms gently. I lay back, trying to relieve the throbbing pain down my spine.

"Dearie, you've no need to worry. I just had a funny turn, and the hospital was trying to tick all their boxes." She smiled. "Oh, and while I'm thinking about it, I haven't had the chance to tell you properly...Frank and I would never have allowed you to go into that nursing home. And you certainly won't be homeless. You can come to Whitebridge Sands. Our only hold-up was making sure you'd have suitable care and accommodation."

"Thank you, Aunt Bella. I don't know where I'd be without you."

"How's everything been going here?" she asked.

"The treatment programme's hard going, but I'm putting my all into it. I've had a few appointments with the occupational therapist. We're working on building a gradual routine, adjusting my goals, and breaking them down into small chunks – alongside pacing, et cetera. I know I keep repeating this: my one goal is to return to my career." I paused. "But I've had an email from my proofreading line manager, saying they've terminated my contract."

Unable to contain my tears, I pulled up the thin blankets to cover my body, hiding my face in the pillow to muffle my sobs.

"Oh, dearie, you're being far too hard on yourself."

"I am so disappointed in myself." I blew my nose on a tissue Aunt Bella gave to me and took a deep breath. "I've been unable to keep up with their demands, even though it's less than part-time."

"It's time to concentrate on you and your well-being. The rest will come."

"The most frustrating part of being here is that some of the staff think all my symptoms are the result of psychological trauma. I had an argument with one of the nurses, who attempted to talk me out of taking my pain relief. I don't have an addiction or dependence on pain relief medication. I am in chronic, severe pain. I need relief to enable me to function and have a quality of life. Why is that so difficult for people to understand?"

"Do you want me to have a word? I'm not having you being denied the medication you need." Aunt Bella thumped her fist on the bedside table.

"Thank you, but it's OK at the moment. I'm still receiving my medication."

"OK. As long as you're sure. How is your dad doing?"

"Dad's doing well. The staff have been great at keeping me informed. They feel he'll need to stay at least another month, but with support from the Community Stroke Rehabilitation Team – especially with speech and language therapy and physiotherapy, he'll be able to be discharged back home. To where he thinks I still live. I wonder how Emma will get out of that one?"

"She's pure evil. When your dad's well enough, he'll see the truth."

"I certainly hope so. Anyway, I've had some happiness recently. A beautiful person called Tina has been visiting me."

Aunt Bella raised her eyebrows, and I explained.

"We met on social media. Every time she's come, she's brought a picnic for us. We're getting to know each other, and it's lovely. Conversation is even easier in the real world than it was online. She makes me belly laugh. It's been such a long time since I literally laughed out loud."

Aunt Bella scrunched up her lips and made a kissy face.

"Stop it, Aunt Bella." I laughed. "For the first time in several years, I feel a sense of hope. I hope Tina will want to stay in my life for many years to come."

"I'm so pleased for you. She sounds lovely."

Frank and Melody walked into my room, and by their body language alone, I knew there was something amiss.

Melody's face looked swollen, and she seemed unable to stand still.

"Melody, are you OK?" I asked. Her eyes glanced towards me for only a second before looking back down at the ground.

"Don't you think you should be asking Grace that?" Frank asked Melody.

I raised my eyebrow. I'd never heard Frank speak to Melody like that before.

"Good luck today, Grace. I really hope it goes well for you." I turned to see Rebecca leaning against my open door.

"Thank you. I'll see you tonight." I smiled.

Aunt Bella turned to me. "Yes, let's get cracking. We've got quite a drive, Gracey."

~

"Grace Braxton?" a male voice announced.

"Yes, I am here."

Frank pushed me towards the reception area, and I took a long, deep breath.

"Please go to Room 5. Are you all going in with the patient?" the receptionist asked.

"Yes, we are dearie," Bella replied.

"Were the hospital OK with you going to this appointment?" Frank asked me.

"I just said I had a medical appointment; I didn't go into detail, and they have no problem with any patient going to other appointments as long as it doesn't interfere with their treatment programme," I explained.

An athletic-built young woman bent down to shake my hand. "Hello there. I am guessing you must be Grace?"

"Hello, Dr Pinewood. Thank you for seeing me."

The doctor guided us all into her consulting room.

"Please take a seat, Grace's family." Dr Pinewood leaned on her desk.

The doctor's consulting room was full of sporting

trophies, army-style photos, and aggressive motivational quotes. I gripped my fists into a ball.

"Grace, I can tell you one thing for certain, we are going to get you out of that chair!"

"That would be wonderful." I cleared my throat. "How would you do that? I tried to find more detailed information on your treatment programmes, and I could only find small details. But the reviews from chronic illness patients are amazing. That's why I wanted to see you."

"Well, there is a reason I do not reveal all about my treatment programmes," she said. "I am a doctor, but I am also running a business. I do not want people stealing my ideas, and some patients are not always keen on my methods. But as you can see, I get results! I meet patients to show them how I'll cure them."

"So just to find out about the programme, a patient has to pay you a huge amount of money?" Aunt Bella said.

"If Grace does the best thing for her health and comes on this programme, then the money for this appointment will be knocked off her treatment bill." Dr Pinewood forced a smile.

"What is the treatment programme, then?" Grace asked.

"The first two to three weeks is educational. We show you what chronic fatigue and chronic pain really is. We show you that you are the one who keeps those symptoms going in your body, and we show you how to change your diet and your lifestyle. We wean you off those medications you don't need. And then the remaining six weeks, it is a military-style rehabilitation. We'll get your body working, shock it back in to shape. Get you out of your chair for good! At the end of the day, Grace, your scans show nothing is wrong with you. We just need to snap you out of it!" Dr Pinewood snapped her fingers.

I gripped the hand rests of my wheelchair with such force, my hands almost got cramp. My entire body began to shake, and bile rose throughout my body until it reached my mouth.

"Go to hell!" I screamed so loud that I couldn't hear anything else around me.

I burst into tears as Aunt Bella, Frank, and Melody wheeled me out of the consultation room. Staff came rushing towards us, looking towards the smug doctor for orders.

"Remove these people. She's obviously psychotic," Dr Pinewood demanded.

"How dare you!" Melody shouted. "My sister's a wonderful person, and all she's trying to do is to get better." She took a breath. "She wants to go back to work. Back to the career she's worked so hard for. Can't you see how much it means to her?"

The staff looked on as she continued. "I've never known anyone in my life who has worked as hard as Grace. Now more than ever I can see how much of a crap sister I've been. But you! You're a qualified doctor. Aren't you under some kind of code of ethics? A doctor must take all possible steps to alleviate pain and distress. Yet, you seem to think that putting my sister – who's in agony and wheelchair-bound – into an army training camp is a wise medical decision?"

I stared at her in complete wonder.

Frank, Aunt Bella, and the people in the waiting room all clapped their hands and nodded their heads in agreement. The staff stood back, avoiding eye contact with the doctor.

Melody's eyes widened as she attempted to hide behind Aunt Bella. But she changed her mind and took a big deep breath and walked towards me. She sat beside me on bended knee and gently wiped my tears away.

"I am sorry for everything, Grace. I know I've said this before, but I'm going to be a much better sister from now on – if you'll have me?"

"Mel, come here."

She pulled me into a tight hug. Noticing me flinch, she softened her grip and held me like I was a fragile puppy.

My broken heart began to mend.

18

FRANK HOLTON

APRIL 2017

I ran my hand through my hair and pulled it tight, taking a deep breath as I looked at the scene of devastation around me. The specialist cleaners had salvaged what they could of the cat sanctuary staff room, but it still looked like a bomb had hit it. An acrid and unpleasant smell remained.

"Here you are, son." Aunt Bella passed me a cup of tea and a homemade slice of orange fluff cake she had brought over from the house. The warm tea soothed my throat and nerves.

"At least there are no structural problems, and after these specialists have finished, the kitchen fitting people can start, and everything will be operational again." Aunt Bella wiped the crumbs off her daisy-print vintage dress.

"I'm really worried about the sanctuary's budget. Will we have enough to cover the repairs?" I asked.

Aunt Bella nodded, but I was worried. "At least the fire was confined to the kitchen, and no one was hurt." I rubbed my thumping temples.

"Stop being a worrying walnut. I've got insurance, and

I'll be able to get it sorted through them." She wagged her finger at me.

"I can't believe Melody's been so selfish." My body tensed.

"We both know that this is more than the fire. You've had Melody on a pedestal for so long, and now she's fallen so badly everyone can see her knickers!"

I shook my head at the image.

Aunt Bella gently patted my leg. "She's still Melody, and I am not excusing her behaviour, son, but she's so lost in her own thinking and her perception of the world, her mind is on overdrive. Maybe her actions are on impulse."

"I get that, and you know how I feel about her, but she's got to take some responsibility. I know I sound like a bastard, and I should be more kind because of what she's going through, but I can't keep doing this. Especially money-wise, Aunt Bella. She's not paying towards anything. We can't keep carrying her like her dad did. It's not doing her any good, and we won't be able to survive through it, either." I felt sick thinking about the budgets.

"We will have a meeting this afternoon. Have one of them intervention meetings I've seen on one of my programmes." Aunt Bella stood and reached out her hand to mine. "Come on now, son, we can sort this as a family."

I squeezed Aunt Bella's hand in response. My body started to relax, and I grinned. She might be bossy, wear outrageous dresses daily, and force me to eat sugar-filled cakes on a regular basis, but I could never see my life without her.

Aunt Bella, Margaret, Melody, and I were all sitting on the sofa in my living room. Melody sat between us, stroking Milly, who was contentedly purring, and looking up at her with love.

"When your dad and I first spoke about you living here, he was going to pay your way, Melody, until you could support yourself. Or if you found it too much, you could go back home. Obviously, with you saying no at first, and then your dad becoming very unwell, things have changed. Don't get me wrong, we want to support you, but I've had to fund everything myself, and I can't continue to do that," I explained.

"We still want to support you, dearie, and we are so proud of how you stood up for Gracey, but we have come to a point where decisions need to be made. We can't keep coasting along," Aunt Bella said, placing her arm around Melody's shoulders.

I continued. "If you really feel you are unable to work, then we will support you with the benefit applications like we have said before."

Melody's eyes filled with tears.

"No judgement," I said, "if you want to pick that option. But remember you will need to give some of that money for your upkeep."

Margaret placed a plate in front of Melody.

"Cupcake, dear?"

In answer, Melody placed an entire cupcake inside her mouth and began chewing slowly.

"Or we need to talk about your employment at the sanctuary..." I muttered, but Melody held her hand up to stop me talking.

When she'd swallowed the cake, she took a long deep

breath and sat up straight. Margaret, Aunt Bella, and I sat on the edge of our seats.

"I am scared to death, and I don't know how – but I – I want to feel better. I want to do better. I'm sick of feeling like this, and I hate how I am treating people I care about." Melody paused. "I'd like to ask my GP to put my name down for therapy. And Frank, whatever you think regarding work, I will put my everything into it. I will make this up to you, to all of you."

She looked at us, searching our faces for a response.

A wave of admiration washed over me. Her honesty, her vulnerability, and that flicker of determination in her eyes spoke volumes. This was the courageous Melody I knew, fighting her inner battles, and it only deepened my love for her.

"Are you sure about this, dearie? We all want the best for you, including beautiful little Milly here." Aunt Bella stroked Milly's fur.

"Yes, I am as sure as I will ever be. I just thought if I moved here, going back into the world, you know, I wouldn't be able to cope, and I would need to run back to my dad – and I know I haven't been a great daughter, either. And, well, I would just mess up like I do with everything." Melody dropped her chin to her chest. "I just shut myself down and want to do anything to take these awful thoughts and feelings away." She began tapping both of her legs rapidly, forcing Milly to jump off her lap.

I rushed over to Melody, bending down beside her, and I placed my arms around her. Melody squeezed me tight. Her warm tears fell on to her cheeks. I never wanted to let her go.

"We definitely need to talk more in our family, don't you think, Margaret?" Aunt Bella said.

"Yes, and eat more of these divine cupcakes!" Margaret replied.

"Son, I don't mean to interrupt, but would you help me in the kitchen, please? I brought some food to cook us all dinner, and I don't fully understand the fancy buttons on your oven," Aunt Bella said.

I gently took myself away from Melody's embrace and saw Aunt Bella grinning, while lifting a bag of shopping.

"So, you set the temperature here..." I pointed to the oven.

"Yeah, yeah I know all that, son. I just wanted to talk to you for a moment." Aunt Bella sat on the kitchen stool.

"Are we not cooking dinner then, Bella? I am starving." Margaret grabbed the items out of the bag and placed them on the kitchen counter.

"Yes! But your belly will have to wait." Aunt Bella waved her finger.

"Son," she went on, "I know money is a problem, but I don't think we should waste this opportunity. I'll help you with money for Melody. Let's get her the therapy she needs privately."

Margaret began chopping the onions. "And despite the latest incident," she said, "Melody is doing a good job at the sanctuary. Especially helping with things that your Aunt Bella struggles with, like the cleaning, carrying, and paperwork – as well as general looking after the fur babies."

"You never told me you were struggling, Aunt Bella. I knew something wasn't right."

"I am fine. Stop ya fussing!" Aunt Bella rubbed my back.

"Are you sure you are telling me everything?" I asked. "Please don't lie to me!"

"The hospital was being overcautious; I had a dizzy spell

and fell. I've got high blood pressure. Who hasn't these days?" Aunt Bella rolled her eyes.

"You're taking your medication, aren't you, Bella?"

By now, Margaret was heating the onions in the pan, the caramelised aroma making my stomach rumble.

"Yes, of course. Anyway, let's get back to important matters. Please consider my suggestion, son. Let's get Melody therapy privately so she can access the help she needs asap."

"I won't put too much garlic in. I might get some smooches tonight on my date," Margaret said as she continued the cooking preparation.

Aunt Bella and I smiled.

"It sounds like a great plan, and thank you, Aunt Bella, but no, I won't take your money."

"Shush now, son, and get a move on. Tell Melody how you feel about her. I've seen a delightful gown in town that I would love to wear for your wedding." Aunt Bella chuckled.

"Calm down, we've not even kissed, never mind get married." I laughed, but I felt a warm glow, picturing Melody in a wedding gown. I knew she'd look stunning.

"We could kiss now?"

All three of us turned to the doorway of the kitchen with a gasp.

My heart was beating like an express train – not in fear, but in the anticipation of finally kissing my babycake's lips. My feet barely touched the ground as I placed my hands around her beautiful face, and our lips met. Everything around me disappeared, and I was filled with a magnificent feeling of happiness.

It was a happiness born not just of desire, but of a profound connection to her gentle soul, her quiet resilience, and the unique way she made the world feel brighter just by being herself.

Aunt Bella broke the romantic spell. "No pornos in the kitchen, please, kids!"

And we all burst out laughing.

19
GRACE BRAXTON
APRIL 2017

Sitting beside me on my hospital bed, Tina wrapped her arms around me. I rested my head on her chest while her hand caressed my hair. A wave of love and happiness washed over me, a feeling I'd missed for so long.

Tina chuckled as we watched *Notting Hill* together on the laptop. "This is one of my favourite films," she said.

"Yes, it's a good one." I smiled.

Tina visited me every other day. She brought me tasty food, movies, and books. But the best part was the conversations we had for hours. I always enjoyed seeing her. I'd started to fall in love with her, but still wondered what she saw in me.

"How are you feeling after that awful appointment?" Tina asked.

"I'm still blown away by how Melody stood up for me. We're not like we used to be years ago, but she's asking how I am. She's interested in how I'm getting on."

Tina nodded. "That's good."

"It is," I said. "I'm genuinely beginning to enjoy our conversations again. I can still tell her demons are there under the surface. She's so easily distracted. She's always scanning her options for her perceived safety. Yet, it is a positive step in the right direction."

"Definitely," Tina agreed.

I smiled. "And even though once again another medical professional treated me like I was insane, it was such a relief to be genuinely believed by my sister."

"You're so strong, Grace; I'm glad Melody's finally seeing how wonderful you are. How's it been at the unit the past few days?"

"Very intense, to be honest," I said, exhaling slowly. "The physiotherapist is supporting me to take steps safely with a walking frame. I grip onto the handlebars for dear life as I try to lift my feet instead of dragging them. The pain's always excruciating, like I'm stepping on hot coals. I get so far, but then I feel faint, the sweat pours off me, and my body won't allow me to go any further."

"Gosh," Tina said.

"It's not easy. The pain will apparently reduce the more I do the programme here, but it certainly doesn't feel like it yet."

"Sounds very painful, but I admire your determination." Tina kissed me on the top of my head.

"Thank you. I received an email from the newspaper, by the way. Remember I told you about those emails and letters I sent before I was admitted, asking for help? Well, this was their response."

I handed Tina my phone.

Dear Grace,

Thank you for your email and letter.
We are sorry to hear about your current difficulties,
but we feel we cannot publish your story at this time.
We wish you the best of luck.
Kind regards,

K. Miles
North Litten Newspaper

Tina's face went pale as she read the email, and she quickly gave me my phone back.

"Is everything OK?" I asked.

"Yes, sorry, it's just so bad how they've dismissed you like that."

"No one seems interested. I'm just worried because the days are going by, and I am nowhere near cured. I know Aunt Bella said she'll help, but she's got a lot on her plate as it is."

"Just keep trying and thinking positive, beautiful," Tina said.

"Yeah, I guess." Frustration bubbled through my veins. As much as I adored Tina, she didn't seem to fully understand my situation.

Melody rushed into my room with a huge grin on her face.

"Melody! Hi." I lifted myself slowly from Tina's embrace.

"Grace, you won't believe this. Your short story and Frank's photo about Aunt Bella's latest cat have gone viral!" Melody handed me her mobile phone.

"What? Really?" My heart lifted as I read the social media reactions.

"Thousands of people read your story, liked it, and shared it. Some even donated money to the sanctuary. They said your story was touching and inspiring. And Frank's photo is stunning," Melody said.

Tina pecked me on the lips.

"Well done! I told you that you were talented, beautiful." Tina climbed off the bed.

"Thank you." I blushed.

"Aunt Bella is so happy. There hasn't been this much interest in the sanctuary for a long time," Melody said.

"This is wonderful news." *Maybe I am still of use...*

"Melody, it's a pleasure to finally meet you." Tina shook Melody's hand.

"Yes, you too. I've heard a lot about you." Melody sat on my bed and avoided eye contact.

"Does anyone fancy a drink?" Tina asked. "I'm going to get a can from the machine."

Melody and I shook our heads.

On Tina's way out, she ran into Rebecca, and they greeted each other in passing.

Taking a seat in my room, Rebecca said, "I hope you don't mind me popping in for a moment."

"No, of course not," I said. "I believe you've met Melody briefly?"

Rebecca smiled at her. "Hi, Melody. Nice to meet you properly."

"Nice to meet you, too, Rebecca."

"I really don't want to cause any trouble, but I've some concerns about Tina that I really feel you should know about." Rebecca looked at the doorway, then back at me.

"What do you mean?" My heart started to race.

"Before coming to see you, she was asking me and another patient invasive questions. Some of them were quite rude."

"Can you give me some examples?" I asked.

"She was asking in-depth questions about our health conditions – what treatments we've had. Do we believe we are unwell? Do we benefit from being unwell? I found it offensive."

My head was racing, going through any possible reason that might cause her to ask such things.

"Grace, I was going to bring this up before, but there is no teacher listed under Tina's full name at the school you said she worked for. I looked it up on the school's website last night," Melody said.

"I...don't understand. Hopefully, there's some kind of explanation? But I'm sorry you went through that, Rebecca. I will – I'll get to the bottom of it," I stuttered.

"That's OK. I'm more concerned about you," Rebecca said.

One of the care assistants popped her head through the doorway.

"Grace, I have a message from Tina. She had to leave urgently, but she will message you later."

"OK, thank you."

Melody squeezed my hand.

Melody left an hour ago to help at the cat sanctuary, and Rebecca returned to her room.

I recognised the shrill voices coming from the corridor,

and I held on tightly to the bed grab rail to heave myself into a sitting position. Pain rocketed straight through my spine, causing me to take several deep breaths.

"Grace! Here you are. We're so pleased to see you, aren't we, George?"

Grandma Ida and Grandpa George both kissed the side of my cheek.

"Yes, very pleased. Hello, Grace. I am sorry it's taken us so long..." Ida shooed George away with a wave of her hand.

"Yes, I'm sorry we haven't been in touch sooner. We've had an awful time of it all, and we only got your letter last week." Ida sat on the chair beside my bed, all the time fussing with her dress.

"Are you both OK? What's happened? Dad and I were worried that we'd not heard from you." I adjusted the bed into a seating position.

A healthcare assistant brought an additional chair into my room.

"Thank you, Nurse. Two cups of tea would be lovely, thank you." Ida snapped her fingers.

"Grandma! This is not a café." I bundled my fist in the blanket. I had forgotten how rude she could be.

"Don't worry. Would you like a cup of tea, chick?" The healthcare assistant smiled.

"Yes, please. Thank you."

George gingerly sat down beside Ida. "Your grandma will explain," he said.

Grandma Ida nodded and began.

"In our beautiful Spanish home, we didn't have a letter box – same as other properties in the area. You had to go to the local post office and obtain your mail via a lockable box," she explained.

George twisted his newspaper. "But we were chucked

156

out of our home and had our house and post office keys taken away from us."

"Yes, George, I am speaking. Our so-called friend, who we were renting from, basically threw us out, saying he and his family were thrown out of their home, so he needed the property back. We went to the authorities, but they were no help to us." Ida smoothed down her dress.

"They don't like the British, Grace," George said.

"George, don't be racist." Ida tapped George's leg. "We were in such a rush and a panic – packing our belongings and finding temporary accommodation. We couldn't even find our mobile phones or passports for a while, because everything was just chucked into boxes. It was only due to the kindness of our ex-friend's wife that she allowed access to our mail. That made our minds up, didn't it, George?" Ida nodded at him.

"Yes, we have moved back to good old England." George smiled. Something unusual to see on his normally miserable face.

"Oh my goodness. Can't they be prosecuted for that?" I asked. "Surely that's against the law?"

"We've made our peace with it, Grace. Seeing your father has put everything into perspective." Ida's eyes started to fill with tears, but she quickly wiped them away with her handkerchief.

"So you've seen Dad? In hospital?"

"Yes, I'm so sorry we weren't here sooner, but Emma's doing a wonderful job looking after him. I'm glad he has a good wife." Ida and George turned to look at each other and smiled.

"What!" I shouted.

They turned to look at me.

"As soon as Dad was admitted to hospital, she got rid of

me and Melody; she made us homeless!" I bunched the blanket in my fist.

"Come on, Grace, I never had you down for telling nasty tales. I know you and your sister never liked Emma, and she'll never replace your mother, but your dad loves her, and we need to respect that." Ida and George both nodded in unison.

"You honestly think I'd lie about something like that?" My voice cracked. I let go of the blanket and rested my head back on the pillow, staring at the clinical ceiling.

What was the point in fighting? The Wicked Witch of the East Midlands had already won.

"She's having the whole house decorated and revamped for when your father's discharged. We didn't get to see the inside – Emma said it wasn't too safe because of the building work. Very thoughtful of her. But the outside looks beautiful. Fresh paint and beautiful flowers, wasn't there, George?"

"Great…" I muttered, taking a long, slow breath.

Was Dad believing Emma's lies, or would he believe Emma's lies when he saw his revamped home? I grimaced inwardly. *I shouldn't be so selfish.* If Dad was happy and he was getting everything adapted for him, I knew I shouldn't interfere.

"Anyway, I know we haven't been here very much for you and Melody, but we want to try and make that up to you. Melody, Frank, and delightful Bella have updated us on the situation. To cut a long story short, we're good friends with a GP who's married to a pain consultant – top in his field, apparently. We gave him details of your case, and he really thinks he can help you. So we have booked and paid for the appointment. We'll take you, and let's see if we can get this awful pain sorted."

I turned my head slowly to Ida and George, wiped away

stray tears from my cheeks, and wondered if I'd just misheard what was said.

"Do you mean that?"

"Yes, we do, love. We want to help you." George handed me a hospital letter.

20

MELODY BRAXTON

APRIL 2017

Grace and I had a text conversation.

> Hey Mel. I've just spoken to Dad; he appears a lot
> happier in himself, and his stroke rehab nurse said
> that he's improving all the time.

> —That's great news. I sent him a knitted colourful
> jumper that I found online from the both of us. I
> thought it would make him smile.

> That's thoughtful of you, thank you, Mel. How are
> you feeling?

> —I'm so happy with Frank. I never thought in a
> million years that he wanted me in a relationship
> way. You were right all along; I wish I'd never pushed
> my feelings down all those years ago, but thankfully
> they've surfaced very easily.

I knew you two would get together, eventually. Got to go, speak later.

$$\sim$$

"It's been a big day for you, babycakes."

Frank brought my hands to his lips and kissed them. Though I'd known Frank nearly all my life, the butterflies in my stomach felt like we'd just met.

"How do you feel the appointment with the doctor and your first therapy session went?" Frank asked as he started the car.

"The doctor was nice. She has changed my medication to see if it will help me. She said it can take about four weeks to get into my system. Therapy was fine, but I feel like l could sleep for the rest of the day now." I leaned my head against the car doorframe, trying to keep myself awake. "I have got some homework to do. Journal writing, thought records, and some relaxation exercises," I explained, looking through the documents from the therapist.

"Do you feel OK to do them?" Frank asked.

"Yes, I'll give them my best shot."

My heart felt so full of love that I couldn't help but smile. I still couldn't believe that this beautiful man was in love with me – and that he had been for many years. For so long, I buried my feelings for Frank to protect myself. The pretty girls were always after him. I thought I had to find other ways to obtain love.

"Don't worry if you want to catch twenty winks, babycakes."

I closed my eyes, but I didn't fall asleep. Instead, I went over some of the things my therapist said to me.

"You must be an active participant in therapy; you can't be

a passenger, otherwise it'll never work. I want you to get the most out of your time here. I believe in your ability to get through this. We'll work together to find ways to help you cope and heal."

I jolted myself upright with that thought. Glancing over at Frank, I noticed the deep bags under his eyes. He reached into the cup holder for his large energy drink.

"You look really tired, darling. Are you OK?" I asked.

"Yeah, I am good. By the way, has Patrick stopped bothering you now? I blocked Lilly."

Patrick had been texting me for weeks, whenever he was aroused and bored. Even though I'd been hesitant and had hovered over the Block button, I'd sighed with relief when it was done.

"Are you OK, babycakes?" Frank asked.

"I blocked him, darling, like we agreed."

Frank smiled broadly.

"I can still win!" Frank laughed.

I placed my hands tighter over his eyes and wrapped my legs around his lower back.

"You will not beat my high score." I giggled then nibbled his ear.

"I master this game, even with your cheating." Frank took one of his hands off his game controller and, reaching behind his back, began to tickle me.

Laughing hysterically, I removed my hands from his eyes and tickled him back in defence.

"Look who just won the championship." Frank burst out laughing.

"Nooo!"

With my legs still entwined around his body, Frank managed to swivel around to face me.

He gently brushed a lock of hair out of my eyes.

"My beautiful babycakes, I love you so much," he whispered in my ear.

The alluring warm cinnamon scent of his aftershave aroused me.

His wonderful lips meshed with mine, and he placed his hand behind my head, locking us close. His other hand travelled down my body, and my core flooded with warmth.

Before I knew it, I was lying on the floor with this godlike man on top of me. He kissed each inch of my body like I was the most mouth-watering pleasure he'd ever had. A blissful light-headedness overcame me as I succumbed to his caresses.

Nestled in Frank's loving arms, I was slightly out of breath – he was, too. Covered in my favourite Milly photo blanket, with the real Milly sitting on top of us, purring, I smiled and hugged Frank tighter, completely happy.

"Why do you call me *Babycakes*?" I asked.

"Don't you remember? I'd signed up to do a photography course after I'd finished school. When my parents found out, they went crackers and told me I had to put everything into the hotel. Any training should be for the hotel, not my silly hobby. Do you remember how devastated I was?"

"Yes, I do. Me and Grace were staying at our grandparents' old caravan park. Grace was trying to make a presentation for you to persuade your parents to change their minds and I..." I hesitated.

Frank continued for me. "You listened to me, talked to me, and hugged me for hours – even days on end, just like you did every time I couldn't cope with my parents' pressure." Frank kissed the top of my head. "And every time I was upset, you'd try to bake my favourite cupcakes, but you'd never quite get the hang of it. They always turned out to be tiny balls of chocolate chips, overcooked cake mixture, and icing."

"They were not overcooked, just a different style of baking!" I poked Frank in his side, and he laughed.

"Either way, I always looked forward to the babycakes." Frank lifted my head towards his and gently kissed me.

Staring into his beautiful eyes, I said, "I'm sorry I've not been there for you, darling, in recent years. I feel awful. I should have been more supportive of you, especially since your parents died."

"Babycakes, you've been to hell and back. I'm going to support you every step of the way."

"Same to you, darling."

"Hello, you love birds. Come on in – make yourself at home." Aunt Bella hugged us both in a warm embrace. Her onesie's fluffy hood tickled my nose.

"I think this is the first time I've not seen you in one of your beautiful dresses, Aunt Bella," I said.

"I like to be cosy in the evening, and I still think these are fabulous. Roar!" Aunt Bella curled her hand, pretending to be a lion.

"I'll start worrying when I see Aunt Bella in a plain track suit." Frank laughed.

Aunt Bella guided us into the living room. I'd been to this house several times, though I'd only ever been in the kitchen, dining room, or the cat sanctuary. There was always a comforting aroma of lavender throughout the house. It was unusual to see Aunt Bella in a more relaxed atmosphere.

"Margaret, the kids are here. Put the kettle on," Aunt Bella called into the kitchen.

Slumping down onto the sofa, she yawned. Several ginger cats were curled up close to the fireplace, two older cats were sleeping peacefully in matching cat beds, and the entire living room was cluttered with cat ornaments and beautiful photos.

I sat on a rug on the floor, fussing the adorable ginger cats.

"I love your living room, Aunt Bella. It's gorgeous," I said.

"Thank you, dearie. My wonderful home and sanctuary is all thanks to my Jim." Aunt Bella stared at a photo.

Frank sat next to Aunt Bella and placed his hand over hers.

"I'm so pleased you took these wonderful photos of my Jim and me, son. They really do capture our happy memories." Aunt Bella squeezed Franks hands and smiled.

"Frank took these cat photos too," she said, looking at me. "It's like we're in a professional photography gallery, isn't it?"

"They are fantastic, darling!" I reached out to briefly touch Frank's knee.

"I'm so pleased that your photos and Gracey's stories are bringing more attention to the sanctuary. I really wish you'd do more of your photography, son. Your face lights up when you take your wonderful photos," Aunt Bella said.

"Hello, kids! We've had another hectic day. Goodness me, it's non-stop with your Aunt Bella," came a familiar voice.

Margaret walked in, wearing a unicorn onesie. Frank and I both suppressed a laugh but couldn't help smiling. She placed a tray of goodies in front of us, then sat down on the other side of the table.

"Help yourself, everyone. Fresh fudge brownies from the local bakery," Aunt Bella said.

Frank and I both looked at each other with raised eyebrows.

"So, this morning we went to help at the community centre, then we did some shopping. We cleaned the cat sanctuary, looked after the cats, and then prepared outfits for my band's upcoming shows. We are such a good team, aren't we, Bella?" Margaret slurped on her tea.

"Absolutely, Margaret. So, Mel, are you happy with everything we discussed the other day? You're happy with what you're doing at the sanctuary? Of course, if I am not here, you can always get either me or Margaret on the phone."

Remembering how hectic it could be, my stomach churned. Frank smiled at me encouragingly.

"Yes...Yes, I am. Thank you for your support, Aunt Bella."

A furious knocking nearly made me jump out of my skin. Even the cats hid under the sofa.

"Don't worry, kids, it's probably someone demanding we take their cats in," Margaret said as she got up to answer the door.

"I'll go, Margaret. You stay here." Frank stood beside Margaret, puffing his chest out.

"We handle this stuff all the time, son. You sit yourself down." Aunt Bella gently pulled at Frank's arm as Margaret left the room.

Soon, a loud, screeching voice was echoing throughout the house.

"Where is Frank? I need to speak to him. It's urgent. Get out of the way, you stupid old woman!"

Aunt Bella and Frank rose from the sofa like a pair of jack-in-the-boxes.

"Oh, it's you! Get out of my house, Mrs No Knickers. You're not welcome here." Aunt Bella stood to face Lilly.

"I doubt you'll be saying that for much longer, seeing as I'm growing a new addition to your family." Lilly clicked her fingers in Aunt Bella's face.

"No…" I whispered. My heart was pounding, sweat drenching my skin. *Please, let this be nothing but a nightmare.*

"What the hell are you talking about?" Aunt Bella spat.

"Before your precious Frank dumped me for that fat lump over there, we were at it like rabbits, and I never was great at taking the pill every day." Lilly sneered at me.

"You're a liar!" Frank grabbed Lilly's arm, turning her nasty Barbie face away from me.

Lilly shoved a letter into Frank's chest.

"I asked my doctor for a positive pregnancy test letter, so that should give you all the evidence you need." Lilly smirked.

21

GRACE BRAXTON

APRIL 2017

"It's nice to see you in the communal room more often, Grace. I bet it gets boring being in your room so much," Rebecca said.

"Yes, it's nice for a change of scenery," I said. "I had a phone conversation with Aunt Bella earlier today. She seemed preoccupied, but that's usual around the anniversary of her husband's passing. I suspect she adopts this flurry of activity as a means to cope. However, I can't help but worry about the toll it takes on her, particularly considering her recent hospitalisation."

"I'm sure she's OK. Maybe she just needs time to distract herself, like you said."

I thought about that for a moment. "Perhaps," I said. "And when I mentioned that my discharge was imminent, the news elicited little reaction."

I told Rebecca that I'd had a conversation with Frank as well. He'd enquired about my well-being and had offered to bring anything I might need, which was thoughtful.

But like with Aunt Bella, at the point in the conversation

when I'd brought up my nearing discharge, Frank, too, had appeared to be distracted.

"I wouldn't worry," Rebecca said. "I bet they're working on things behind the scenes. I know from what you've told me, they love you to bits."

"Thank you. Oh, and yesterday, I had another MDT meeting. Discharge is a big topic of conversation. They've referred me to North Litten Council. After what you said about being housed in a hostel where people took illegal drugs and were aggressive, the thought of it terrifies me."

"Yes, it was an awful time. The council said I had two choices: stay there or sleep on the streets. The only upside to the hostel was being on the ground floor, but I was too scared to leave my room."

I squeezed Rebecca's arm. I wished there was something I could do for her.

"The MDT team say I've made slight improvements, but they're disappointed. According to them, I should have made greater strides by now. Yet, I'm pushing with every depth of my strength. Some of them roll their eyes when they see me in pain – whether I'm sweating or doubled over, vomiting, it doesn't seem to matter. One of their key messages is pacing. How is pushing my body to the limit *pacing*?" I said, brushing my hair back tightly.

"I totally get what you mean. Some of the staff members here make my blood boil. They've no idea. But at least there are some good ones, too, who genuinely seem to want to help," Rebecca said.

"Yes, you're right. I always love your optimism." I smiled.

"Are you seeing Tina today? How did it go when you confronted her about everything you found out?" she asked.

"We are meeting in the hospital café this afternoon.

She's said she'll explain everything. I feel sick about it, to be honest."

"I'll be thinking about you."

~

"Here you are, love. I'll come back to pick you up in an hour. Is that alright?" the healthcare assistant said as she wheeled me into the hospital café.

"Yes, that's great. Thank you, Anita." I smiled and waved as she headed back to the ward.

I took a deep breath. Fiddling with the straps of my handbag, I tried to block out the constant chatter around me. A wave of nausea washed over me as I spotted Tina in the distance, walking towards me.

"I got us two teas." She placed the cardboard cups down and tentatively sat on the chair opposite me.

"Grace, I don't know how to say this, but I've done this before." She looked to the ground.

"Done *what* before?" I asked.

"I've met several people with chronic illnesses. I've been able to meet them easily online. Then I tell them I've also got a chronic illness to show I can relate to their situation."

"What!"

Before I could say anything else, Tina quickly continued. "But it was different with you. I wanted to spend time with you, and I fell in love with you. You became so much more than a work project."

"A fucking work project! Are you kidding me?"

"I work for a national newspaper. This scoop is a huge opportunity – and could lead to a major promotion. You more than anyone can understand how important that is."

"Let me get this right – you contacted people with

chronic illnesses, fooled them into thinking they can trust you for a story. What the hell is this story?"

"Well, it's an article that asks an interesting question. Is chronic illness a way to escape work and life's responsibilities?"

I stared at her. "You disgust me, Tina. Surely this is illegal."

"Many reporters do undercover work. And let's set the record straight, Grace. When we were together, you were never really one hundred percent with me. You are so obsessed with getting your career back and finding a cure for your illness that you don't look at what you have right in front of you. You don't enjoy what you have: someone who cares about you."

"How many chronic illness sufferers have you led up the garden path?"

"It wasn't like that with any of the others."

"You expect me to believe that you felt something for me? Seriously, after what you've just told me? Rubbish! I always wondered what this intelligent, stunning woman would possibly want with someone like me. You were the one who messaged me regularly and encouraged us to meet. You abused my thinking patterns and my situation."

My eyes pricked with tears. I pushed my fingernails into the wheelchair's arms, causing spikes of pain to rush up my spine.

"Grace, I'm so sorry. I never expected to fall in love with you. I'm sorry for everything."

I held up my hand. "Get away from me, Tina."

I could hardly catch my breath.

Tina walked away from the table as café customers stared at us.

Her words were like vicious kicks to my body. I swallowed hard to stop the tears of anger turning into tears of self-pity. More than anything, I wanted a hug from my dad and Milly the cat.

～

"George, she's tired. She doesn't want to hear about your boring fishing trip." Ida waved George off dismissively. "You should smell him after he's been fishing, Grace. Gracious! It takes me days to get the smell out of the house, but I must allow him to have his hobbies. I know how to keep my husband happy. Don't I, George?" Ida held her head high, smiling smugly.

A burst of laughter escaped my mouth, but luckily, I managed to turn it into a cough. George hid his small grin behind his newspaper.

"Oh dear, I hope you're not coming down with anything. These hospitals are full of bugs, aren't they?" Ida said.

"How's Dad doing?" I shuffled in my wheelchair, trying to find a comfortable position.

"He's doing well; the doctors and nurses seem pleased with him." George smiled, and the knot in my stomach instantly loosened.

"Yes, thank you, George." Ida placed her hand in the air in George's direction.

"He is actually doing marvellously well, Grace. We think he should be home already, but they know best, don't they. Emma's been a true angel. Every time we pass the house on the way to the hospital, more work is being done to it. James will have a wonderful welcome home when he's discharged," Ida explained.

I took a deep breath, smelling the pungent anti-bacterial cleaning products, and looked away from them both.

"You'll be moving back home when you're discharged as well, won't you, Grace?" George asked.

"As I explained, Emma kicked me and Melody out." I turned to face them.

"Not this nonsense again. Please stop this childish behaviour," Ida said.

"Have you even asked Emma about it?" I glared at Ida.

"I think we should confront her. I doubt Grace would lie about such a thing," George added.

"George! She's a wonderful wife to our son, especially in his time of need. I'll hear no more about this." Ida slammed both of her hands on her lap.

"I'm sorry to interrupt, but are you Grace Braxton and co?" A man appeared next to me.

"Yes, I am Grace, and they're my grandparents." The nervous knot in my stomach returned.

"It is a pleasure to meet you, Grace. I am Dr Finlay – Senior Pain Consultant. Please follow me, everyone."

"Thank you for your email, Grace. It is very informative." Dr Finlay smiled.

"I understand from what your grandparents have told me – and from your email – that you've been through an awful time of it, and I do hope we can at least put a plan together to manage your pain as much as possible," Dr Finlay said, keeping steady eye contact.

"That'd be wonderful." The knot turned into a flutter.

"After looking at your scans, appointments, assessments, et cetera – and I've spoken to the unit – I believe your primary diagnosis is severe chronic pain syndrome, which would explain your high levels of pain, and you are most likely exhausted, causing the high level of fatigue. Sadly, it's a harsh cycle. Because of your symptoms, you're losing your core strengths, such as balance and muscle strength, because you're not able to move as much, which will also add to the fatigue."

"What's caused all this, Doctor?" Ida asked. "She was a thriving, ambitious young woman, and then struck down in the prime of her life."

"There are many theories. Some are unkind towards the patient. Many are like Grace, very hard-working, just wanting to get on with life, and then this debilitating condition comes along – life-changing in many circumstances. The most basic answer is seeing chronic pain as a faulty alarm system. The brain is still sending out pain messages, even when there is no threat or harm. Grace's nervous system has become overactive."

"Can't you just fix that, Doctor? Put a new alarm system in Grace's body or something?" Ida asked.

"I really do wish it was that simple," Dr Finlay said.

"Dr Finlay, do you think there's a way for my pain levels to be improved, please?" I asked. "My current pain relief is not helping me much at all."

"Yes, I can see it's not effective and isn't helping your rehabilitation. I would not like you on this medication long term, due to the possible risks, but I do feel it will help you proceed further with the physiotherapy, for example. I want to help with your quality of life and ability to function. I'm going to start you with a low dose of Oramorph four times a day to replace your current medication. I'll contact your unit to inform them, and I'll ask to attend one of your next MDT meetings," Dr Finlay explained.

"So how much will all this cost me, Doctor?" Ida asked.

"I've written a letter for Grace's GP that will instruct them to send an NHS referral to my department. That way, after today, she'll become an NHS patient with me. Therefore, only today will require payment. Would that be OK for you, Grace?" Dr Finlay asked.

Tears of relief streamed down my face. I sighed and exhaled loudly, as if I had been holding my breath for a lifetime. George rushed over to me, hugged me tentatively, and handed me his tissue.

"It's alright, my dear. Everything will be OK."

I held on to George's arm, welcoming the warmth of human contact from someone who cared.

"Thank you. I am really grateful to you, Dr Finlay, and thank you, George and Ida." I let go of George's arm and he walked back to a slightly stunned Ida.

"I'll book you an appointment for four months' time to see how you are getting on." Dr Finlay walked around to me and placed his hand on my shoulder. "We might not get you back to the life you once had, but I will try everything in my power to support you to have the best quality of life possible."

22

BELLA

APRIL 2017

"This doesn't sit right with me, son. I think she's up to something bad." I poured the tea into my mismatched teacups.

"How can you explain the doctor's letter? The dates would make sense if I think about when we were together. Two months pregnant." Frank rubbed his temples.

I sat down next to him and rubbed my hand up and down his back.

"Could it be a fake letter?" Margaret suggested as she shared out the strawberry milk-chocolate cupcakes I'd made last week. I hoped Frank wouldn't notice they weren't fresh today. I placed my hand over my mouth to stifle a yawn.

"It looked pretty genuine to me, and she is shocking with anything to do with technology," Frank explained.

"You have already given her a lot of money, Frank, and the baby is not even born yet," Margaret said.

"Well, she needs maternity clothes and to get a pram and items for the baby," Frank said.

"How are we sure that you're the father, son?" I asked.

"It has crossed my mind, and it's embarrassing to say,

but that was the base of our relationship, you know? Sex." Frank's cheeks turned red.

"Yes, well I imagine she wasn't a great conversationalist. Every time she leaves her home, she is practically showing her unmentionables. Horny devils must fall at her feet," I remarked.

Frank burst into laughter.

"A while ago, I saw Mrs Holloway's grandson with Lilly," I went on. "Nothing happened, I suppose. I was looking out of the community centre's kitchen window. They were talking and it looked like Lilly was flirting. I didn't think much of it at the time."

"I don't think that was anything. They've known each other since school, and Lilly flirts with anything that moves." Frank picked up another cupcake.

"Mrs Holloway would surely have a fit if she knew that her precious grandson was spending time with Lilly," Margaret said.

"Well, you'd have thought so. I often think they're like the royal family of this town. But I do appreciate how much they donate to the community centre."

"There's a paternity test that can be completed while the baby is still in the womb, but apparently it's risky for the baby and mother," Frank said. "So, it'll have to wait until the baby is born. I just can't take the chance of not being there for my possible child, even during Lilly's pregnancy. I know my parents loved me, but they let everything come before loving their child – loving *me*."

I squeezed Frank's hand, remembering how many times I would go to fetch him and find him alone in the hotel reception, hiding under the desk.

"I never understood your parents' way of thinking, son, but I know in their own way they loved you very much."

Frank let go of my hand and pulled me in close for a hug. My heart warmed with love for the boy.

"The next thing is: how in the world are we going to help Melody cope through this?" Margaret asked.

We broke our embrace and sat back in our seats, each of us lost in thought.

~

"I'll have to add 'hot blanket service' to your job description," I said as I found Melody sitting cross-legged on the floor, leaning against Mrs Snowfluff's apartment. The white cat lay peacefully beside her, half curled on Melody's lap.

"Just taking a ten-minute break, Aunt Bella," she said, staring blankly into space.

With a groan, I lowered myself onto the floor next to her, my knees crunching in protest. I leaned my back against the wall.

"I bet this is a lot more comfortable for Mrs Snowfluff than it is for me," I muttered, adjusting my position as every movement made my joints click.

"I knew I didn't deserve happiness. I knew it would all go wrong." Melody's body began to shake with uncontrollable tears, and Mrs Snowfluff darted for cover, slipping under the hem of my dress.

"Listen to me, young lady," I said, reaching out to her. "Frank worships the ground you walk on. He never loved that tart." I squeezed her hand, hoping to ease her distress.

"There's no way I can do this. I just can't!" Melody cried between sobs.

"Don't let that awful girl shatter your dreams. You and Frank are meant to be together, just like me and my Jim." My fingers brushed my wedding ring, and my heart tightened at the memory of him. It was never this complicated for us.

"She's going to be the mother of his child. They're going to share a bond I can't compete with," Melody whispered, snapping the bobbles on her wrist.

"Do you know how many people out there have children with someone they can't stand?" I asked gently. "They do what they can for the child, but it doesn't mean they're in love with the person they had the baby with."

"I kind of thought a baby made everything magical between two people," she said, lifting her head.

"In the movies, maybe. But in real life? A baby only brings happiness when both people put in the effort, with love and trust. Without that, it doesn't work – just like marriage."

Melody's face was swollen and blotchy from crying, and my heart ached for her. I knew I wouldn't always be able to protect her. "Please don't make any rash decisions, dearie. You've been doing so well here. And I'm going to have a hard time finding someone who loves the fur babies like you do, so think of your old Aunt Bella."

She sat up and smiled through her tears. "Thank you, Aunt Bella." We squeezed each other's hands.

Mrs Snowfluff poked her head out from beneath my dress, and I stroked her velvety fur as she purred softly. The calming cadence lulled me into a peaceful slumber.

"Bella! Bella, are you alright?" Margaret asked.

I jolted awake at the touch of Margaret's hand. A shock of pain shot up my back as I attempted to stand.

"It's not like you to fall asleep in the day, especially not in the cats' apartments. Melody came to fetch me." Margaret looped her arm with mine and supported me to stand.

We wobbled like we'd had too many sherries, but our combined elderly bodies did the job.

"I'm perfectly fine, Margaret. I was just doing *mindfulness* or whatever the kids call it." I waved off Margaret's concerns.

"Are you sure? I've been worried about you."

"I'm absolutely sure. Stop your faffing."

"You've got a lot of missed calls from Grace on your mobile. Shall I call her back for you?" Margaret asked.

"Oh fiddlesticks! I haven't called her back in days. I do hope she's OK. She must think awfully of me. I must call her back now." I wiped away a threatening tear as my chest tightened with guilt. I started to rush towards the house when Margaret grabbed my arm.

"The thing is, Bella – we've got the charity concert. We need to be at the community centre in twenty minutes."

"Damn! I forgot all about that, and I didn't even bake the chocolate orange cakes. I was supposed to make several."

"Don't worry. Let's just get going, and we can take the rest of your lovely cupcakes from last week," Margaret suggested with a gentle smile.

"No, no! Definitely not. Not for one of your shows. We'll have to go without, and I'll make my apologies. Let's go."

"Stop flirting and concentrate, Margaret. You're on in five minutes." I jerked my thumb in the direction of the stage.

"I'm sorry, Bella. I can't keep away from this beauty, especially when she looks so naughty." Charles pouted his lips.

"Apart from when you stand her up for someone else. Get away! Shoo!" I waved him away dismissively.

Margaret twirled, her swing dress sparkling with bright colours. She looked fantastic. For once, I was under-dressed in a plain gown.

"I think he really likes me, Bella." Margaret clasped her hands in excitement.

Placing my hands on my hips, I said, "Have you forgotten how he treated you last time?"

"He has apologised relentlessly, says he wants to make it up to me."

"Don't be so stupid. He just wants to get into your knickers." I rolled my eyes.

Margaret allowed a small burst of laughter to escape before quickly placing a hand over her mouth.

"Now, forget about dirty old men like him, and focus on raising money with your brilliant talent."

Margaret hugged me tightly, and I returned her embrace.

"I don't know what I'd do without you, Bella."

"You'd do wonderfully well, Margaret."

Fish, Chips, and Mushy Peas were a raging success. Margaret came alive when she was on stage, and the band did a marvellous cover of 'Let's Get It Started' by the Black-Eyed Peas.

The community centre was packed, with most people dancing and enjoying the entertainment. A delicious waft of chips, hot dogs, and sizzling burgers floated from the kitchen.

"Bella, Margaret, it's lovely to see you both. Fantastic entertainment."

"Mrs Holloway, it's wonderful to see you again. I'm pleased you enjoyed the show," Margaret said.

"I do like to visit the places I make generous contributions to – make sure the money is spent well," Mrs Holloway said with a smirk.

"Rest assured, it surely is here," I said.

"Yes, I can see that. I'm also celebrating. I will soon be a great-grandmother."

"Congratulations! That is such lovely news," Margaret said.

"Yes, I bet you can't wait to meet the bundle of joy," I said.

"I'm so excited, ladies. We had a new professional family photo done recently. I wanted my grandson's fiancée to feel included in the family."

Mrs Holloway produced the photo from her handbag and passed it to us. I grasped the photo, and at that moment, everything around me appeared to come to a standstill.

"Lilly!" Margaret whispered.

"Mrs bloody No Knickers!" I shouted, and everyone looked at us.

"What!"

"Mrs Holloway, this *person* has told my great-nephew that her unborn child is his and has already had a great deal of money from him for apparent expenses," I said.

"Rubbish! Lilly's a fantastic young woman, and she has a highly respectable career as a lawyer. She wouldn't need to scam people out of money."

"A lawyer! She doesn't know how to spell," I spat.

"I've heard enough. I don't know why you're behaving in this disgusting manner, but it'll impact the community centre's funding."

"We're trying to help you. You and your grandson are being scammed. We can prove it to you," Margaret said.

"Get out! Someone, remove these two low-lifes immediately."

Charles and the other volunteers rallied around us.

"Bella and Margaret are part of our family, and we'll not tolerate them being treated in this manner," Charles said.

My heart warmed at their kindness. The tension in my shoulders, which started when I saw the photo of Lilly, suddenly dissipated.

"You'll all regret this. Now, give me my photo back."

Margaret and I exchanged glances.

"Run!" I exclaimed.

I hastily tucked the photo into my bra, and we both fled, moving as clumsily as two people with rather cumbersome bones can.

We managed to reach the car park of the shop opposite.

"Well, that was quite the spectacle," chuckled Charles as he materialised in front of us.

It appeared he'd walked faster than we'd run.

Margaret and I were both extremely out of breath, so Margaret popped into the shop to buy two bottles of water.

"Thank you, Charles. You're a good man for standing up for us," I said, leaning on his arm for support.

Charles delicately stroked my hand, his gaze lingering on mine.

"Bella, you're one of a kind. But I'm worried about you. We all are. You can't look after everyone, and it always seems like you're rushing around with no time to breathe. You even make those young people exhausted just by looking at you."

"Oh, Charles, I'm almost afraid to sit still," I replied.

23

JAMES BRAXTON

MAY 2017

"Thank you all for everything. You're all angels." I handed the staff a large box of chocolates and shook my consultant's hand.

"Yes, thank you for helping our son. We're very grateful to you." George nodded shyly.

"You've done all the hard work, James. It has not been an easy road for you. And remember to keep up your outpatient rehabilitation." The consultant smiled.

I stood tall, using my new walking stick to leave the ward. I turned around to cast one last glance, smiling at a special patient I'd connected with. Then, I took a deep breath. At times, I'd thought I would never leave.

"Brilliant jumper, son. Is that the one your girls sent you?" my father asked.

I smiled, proudly straightening my jumper to display the colourful patterns.

"Yes, that's right, Dad," I replied, noticing Emma roll her eyes.

I had hoped this awful ordeal would bring Emma and the girls together. Obviously not.

"Let's get this show on the road. I can't wait to see what you've done with the place, Emma," my mother said as she walked by my side.

"Don't you think we should give them some time alone, Ida," my father muttered.

"We'll only be with them for an hour, if that, George! You've kept me waiting long enough, Emma, to see this house makeover of yours." My mother wagged her finger in Emma's face.

"Yes, well, I've been very busy, Ida." Emma snarled.

"I know you have, and I've been singing your praises about what a wonderful wife you are to our son."

Emma and my mother exchanged insincere smiles.

"Welcome home, my darling." Emma kissed me on the cheek as we walked into the house.

A strong odour of fresh paint hit me.

"Please go through to the living room. I'll bring through tea and biscuits," Emma said to my parents.

Then she grabbed my arm, nearly taking me off balance before I could join my parents.

She took me to the side. "Now it's time for our life to begin properly, just as we dreamed and talked about," she whispered.

My stomach churned.

"But I'd hoped your speech would have improved by now," she said to me. "We can understand you better, but it's still embarrassing. I hope you're trying with this speech and language therapy."

"I'm trying my best, Emma!"

I heard my mother's voice from the other room. "Oh,

James, this is wonderful! Everything looks so brand new and polished."

"Look at that huge TV!" George shouted.

"Trust you, George," Ida said.

Emma guided me into the living room, and I gasped. It was like a show home. Everything matched, and every part of the room had been replaced with something new.

I gradually lowered myself down onto the sofa, which was very low to the floor. I kept moving positions to attempt to get comfortable, but it was like sitting on a bed of nails. I didn't want to come across as unappreciative, but the only thing I was happy about was that the ghastly canvas of Emma had disappeared.

Emma brought in the refreshments and placed them on the very low, designer coffee table, which was also low to the floor.

"Are you missing my canvas, James?" Emma caught me staring at the opposite wall.

"Don't worry. I have put it in our bedroom. I thought it was more appropriate in there." Emma winked.

"Oh. Yes, great idea, darling," I said, thankful that I would be asleep most of the time in that room.

"Emma, I'm aware that you and James were struggling financially. Have you come into some money?" Ida asked.

"Some things are supposed to be kept private, James. Is anything kept just between us?" Emma's face reddened.

A wave of dizziness washed over me. I reached out and took a sip of my tea to settle my nerves.

"I don't mean to be rude, Emma, and it's very nice-looking – however, I think James will struggle with these low chairs, slippery rugs, and the sharp-edged coffee table. Has the disability equipment arrived yet?" my father asked.

"Unbelievable! You are all so ungrateful!" Emma spat.

"Where did you get this money? This room alone must have cost a fortune," I asked.

"I do all this and the first thing you do is have a go at me! I haven't heard any proper thanks!" Emma stomped her feet, her face reddening with anger.

"We are just asking a valid question, Emma," my mother said.

"James, you took out a large loan behind my back for your daughters, around the time Grace had her little library trip. The loan was approved when you were in the hospital, and I had access to your bank accounts." Emma placed her hand on her hip and smirked.

A sharp chill came over me. The taste of sickness swirled in my mouth, and I gripped the armrest to ground myself.

"Are you telling me that you stole from my son when he was seriously ill in hospital?" My father glared at Emma.

"This is the third time he's taken out a loan without discussing it with his wife first, so I thought – if he continues to behave like a selfish twat, I'll just spend the money on where it should be. On us. Our life, our home, our marriage. Not his bloody lazy daughters!" Emma pushed the matching armchair violently backwards, and it banged against the wall.

I jumped, still trying to ground myself in the room. My father's trembling hand held mine.

My mother stood, placing herself just inches away from Emma's face.

"Grace told me that you kicked her and Melody out of the house. I didn't believe her. But she was telling the truth, wasn't she?"

"I had to start making things happen. You promised me, James, that you would disown your daughters, and it would just be the two of us. I had to terminate our baby because

187

you said it wasn't the right time, and I had to give up my career to have a life with you! You promised me a life of luxury, and all I got were wasted years!" Emma pushed past my mother and leaned towards my now-sweating face, anchoring herself onto the sofa armrest.

"Where are my daughters? Where are they!" I shouted.

I managed to stand up and push Emma back. She lost her balance and tumbled to the carpet.

"We've seen them both, and they're where they say they are, but it means Grace is now homeless," my father explained.

"Don't you even think they're coming back here!" Emma shouted.

"Come on, son, you can come home with us." My parents stood on each side of me, taking hold of my arms to support me. My legs felt like jelly, yet my entire being urged me to help my daughters.

I am so sorry, Melody and Grace. I have let you both down.

I began to feel sick and dizzy again.

"We'll contact the girls and sort this out," my mother said, soothing me as we left the house.

"I'll take you to the cleaners, James. You'll have nothing! And take that ugly disability equipment with you," Emma screamed, pointing at the garage.

24

MELODY BRAXTON

MAY 2017

I lay on my bed, relaxing my muscles. Milly rested on my chest, her gentle purring soothing me. Grace had called me and we were chatting over speaker phone.

"How did it go?" she asked.

"It was great. I set out a nice table on the sand, with Frank's cupcakes, and I had his new camera ready."

"So did he get some good shots, then?"

"He did. He's entered them into Whitebridge Sands Amateur Photographer of the Year Competition."

"I'm so pleased," Grace said.

"Thank you for your help with the planning. He loved it," I said. "You should have seen the smile on his face. He was in his element."

"So, the topic of Lilly and the baby didn't come up, then?"

"Well, there was a moment where I really had to hold back my emotions. Frank just started talking to this random bloke who had his kid with him, and he told him he's looking forward to being a father."

"That can't have been easy to hear, but it won't take away the love he has for you," Grace said.

I held back the tears that threatened to fall and quickly changed the subject.

"Anyway, I'm so relieved that Dad has found out the truth about Emma, and you now have a good home to go to. I know Aunt Bella was doing all she could to find you somewhere here and was fighting numerous obstacles."

"I hope Dad is coping OK as much as he says he is," Grace said. "It's quite a contrast to a few months ago, isn't it? Back then, you couldn't wait to come back to North Litten."

"Yes, you're right there. I'm still stressed, especially with this baby stuff, but I'm feeling better in myself."

"You are doing really well, Mel. I'm so proud of you."

"Thank you. Did you get a chance to reread the Amber Levendale book, by the way?"

"Yes," Grace said. "I finally did this week. I'm in a better headspace to see what she was trying to tell me through her story. I've realised what it is. I don't have to be a successful professional to be a valuable human being. I understand that, but it's hard for me to accept. I still want to make a difference like Mum did."

"We seem to have very different memories of our mother, Grace..."

She ignored my comment.

"Speaking of Amber Levendale," she went on. "When I was packing, I found my Post-it note, reminding me to thank her for her kindness. I've her contact details on a note. I'll do that after this phone call," Grace said.

"Good idea. Before you go, one more thing. Do you think Aunt Bella's OK? Her face looks so much thinner, and she's got large, dark bags under her eyes these days. If I mention anything, she just says she needs time off from baking and dressing like a queen," I said.

"I've been concerned too," Grace said. "She hasn't been in touch as much, but I know the time of the year is difficult for her, you know, the anniversary of Jim's death."

"Oh yes, with all of this worry over Frank and the baby, it had completely slipped my mind. Bless her. Frank and I have missed several calls from her today, being so busy. I must ring her back."

"I hope she's OK. I'll give her a ring as well," Grace said. "Oh, do you remember that photo we found of us all on the beach when we were younger, but Aunt Bella snatched it away? I've been wondering about it."

"I forgot about it, to be honest," I said. "Sorry, Grace, I just heard the front door close. I'll call you back."

Finishing the call, I walked to our bedroom doorway, which gave me a full view of the living room.

My heart sank. Frank and Lilly headed into the living room with shopping bags full of baby items. I'd thought Frank was at work. They sat down together on the sofa.

"I'm so glad we got the 3D scan," Lilly said, unaware that I was watching them. "Look at how adorable our beautiful baby is." She placed the photo on Frank's knees. "You're going to be a wonderful father."

Lilly ran her hand through Frank's hair, and Frank sat back a fraction. He removed Lilly's hand.

"I can't wait to be a father, Lilly, but we're not in a relationship."

Lilly shuffled closer, pressing herself against him. She gently stroked his face. "Remember how much passion we shared. Think about how wonderful it would be if our family were together. You, me, and our baby," Lilly whispered, though not so quietly that I couldn't hear.

Lilly held Frank's hand on her enlarged stomach, and she kissed him passionately.

I started towards them, but my day's intake of food suddenly lurched from my stomach. I shook from head to toe, revolted by the smell. Tears streamed down my face. I couldn't believe what I'd just witnessed.

"Babycakes, are you OK?" Frank was next to me, trying to lift me from the floor.

"Get away from me, you bastard!" I slapped Frank's arms away and steadied myself to a standing position using the facing wall as support.

"You are so pathetic, Melody," Lilly snarled.

"Get out of my house, Lilly. Now!" Frank took her by the arm and firmly guided her to the front door.

"You weren't saying that five minutes ago, lover boy." Walking out of the door, she turned and defiantly blew him a kiss from the doorway.

Frank slammed the door in her face.

I ran back into the bedroom and dragged the suitcase out from under the bed. In a daze, tears so heavy I could barely see what I was doing, I hurled my possessions into it.

"Please let me explain. I love you so much," Frank said, removing items from the bag.

"I believed you, Frank. I actually believed you! I thought you did want me. By some miracle, you were in love with me and wanted us to have a life together. What cruel joke was all this?" I shouted.

"All of those things are true, babycakes. I've no excuse. I lost where I was for the moment. I don't love Lilly – I never have."

I pushed Frank out of the way. He staggered backwards, his face a pale white. I collected all the items that he removed, put them back in the case, and zipped it up.

"Bollocks! Get out of my way."

I dragged my large suitcase to the front door.

"No, please, we can work this out. I know we can. I love you." He begged and gripped my arm. "You're in no fit state to drive."

"I can't stay here anymore. God knows how many times you have been with her since we've been together. You said you were at the hotel this evening." I snatched my arm from his grip.

I walked out. The heavy rain and wind slammed the front door back against the opposite wall.

Frank shouted after me. "I was – until I got a call from Lilly saying she'd had the 3D scan photos done. I felt guilty that I wasn't there for the scan, but nothing has happened. I love you and only you."

I continued to walk to the car, heaved my case onto the backseat, and quickly got inside, locking all the doors.

I looked in the rear-view mirror and saw Frank, soaked and crumpled into a heap on the concrete. Still, I drove away, my heart as frozen as ice.

25

GRACE BRAXTON

MAY 2017

Anita slid my flat purple shoes onto my feet, and I gradually moved my legs back onto the bed. It had taken all morning for me to wash, dress, and present myself in a way I used to before this illness. My muscles ached and the throbbing pain was as exhausting as falling asleep on a clothesline. Yet, as I touched my woven, tailored trouser suit, I felt liberated. I was spending less time in bed, walking more with my crutches, and relying less on my wheelchair. I had recently moved to crutches with the help of the physiotherapist.

I beamed inside. I'd always loved this outfit and never thought I would wear it again.

"You look beautiful, Grace." Anita smiled.

"Thank you for all your help."

"You are most welcome. You have done so well, and I know you'll continue to do so. I think it would be a good idea for you to rest before you go home."

I smiled, wishing I was fully recovered.

"Did the occupational therapist visit your grandparents'?" Anita asked.

"Yes, everything is fine, and we've got disability equipment galore for me and my dad." I laughed.

"Bless you both," Anita replied.

"My latest MDT meeting was a fiery one, but ultimately it went in my favour," I said.

"Really? What happened?" Anita asked.

"You know I told you about Dr Finlay? Well, he was true to his word. He wrote to the unit and attended the meeting," I explained. "The medical professionals involved in my care here weren't keen on prescribing me opioids, but he fought my corner. He said it was unethical to leave me in so much pain and pointed out that I am engaging fully with the treatment. He mentioned that it's so intense for me that I'm often left feeling faint and dripping with sweat from pushing my body to the limit."

Anita nodded. "That sounds tough, but I'm glad he spoke up for you. What was the conclusion?"

"They agreed that the combined methods should be beneficial to me, but they decided to monitor the medication closely. I have so much gratitude for Dr Finlay. He fought for my health and well-being, rather than just following the rule books."

"That's wonderful to hear," Anita said with a smile. "It's rare to find a doctor who truly advocates for their patients like that, and I know I shouldn't say that, working in healthcare."

"Just as Dr Finlay was leaving, he said something that stuck with me," I continued. "He told me, 'Chronic pain is complex. Our pain is unique. There's no one size fits all, but sadly there are still many medical professionals who believe that every patient should fit into criteria boxes.'"

Anita sighed. "Dr Finlay is absolutely right. It's a shame that more doctors don't see it that way."

"Yes, at least I have him on my side. He's given me a renewed sense of hope," I said.

Looking around my room, Anita chuckled and said, "I have no idea how you're going to get all these flowers home. Looks like you've started a florist in here."

"I know. Would I be able to donate them to the ward?"

"I'll check, but I think it will be OK, especially as we're not a traditional medical ward. Did you know pink roses are often associated with love, but they can also be used to express sincere apologies?"

I stared at the bunches of pink roses from Tina, displayed all around the room. They looked beautiful, but my heart was full of hurt. I hated how much I missed her.

Anita grabbed a bag from the chair near the door.

"By the way, two parcels were left for you at reception. I believe one is from Rebecca. I bet you're missing her." Anita handed me the bag.

"Oh, thank you. Yes, I am, but I'm hoping this'll be a positive new start for her."

"By the way, Grace, guess what I saw on my Facebook feed? I believe it was your Aunt Bella's cat sanctuary. A mini story with a photo of one of the cats – and your name was mentioned as the author. I looked at the page, and that was the second viral post. Your post has brought in many donations. You must be so proud."

Before I could answer, Aunt Bella hurried into the room and embraced me warmly.

"I'm immensely proud of her. We've never had so many donations and fans. Thank you, Gracey."

Aunt Bella released me and sat on the side of the bed. At this point, I noticed she was wearing a tracksuit. I'd never seen her wear one in my life.

"I'll leave you both to it. Take care, Grace," Anita said.

"Thank you for everything," I replied.

When Anita had gone, Aunt Bella asked me whether I'd heard from my sister.

"Since yesterday? No, is everything alright?" I asked.

"I swear we're living in an episode of *Coronation Street*," Aunt Bella said. "She moved to your grandparents' place last night."

"What!" I said.

Aunt Bella filled me in on everything that had happened. Including what she'd learned about Mrs Holloway and her grandson.

"I know we should've called them that night, but we were so exhausted after the run. Our old bones aren't used to it. Margaret and I couldn't even manage supper. But we kept trying to reach them as soon as we woke up."

"This isn't your fault, Aunt Bella. I'm just shocked that Frank kissed Lilly in the first place."

"Yes, especially considering how much he loves Melody. But I think his mind was all over the place with this being-a-father business, especially given his childhood and how Mrs No Knickers seems to have some sort of sexual hypnosis over men."

"The worry is, Aunt Bella, who is the father of Lilly's baby? How will we find out?" I asked.

"It must be Mrs Holloway's grandson," Aunt Bella replied. "Lilly was using my boy for his money. Money-hungry cow, but he's going to have it out with her."

I noticed the sheen of sweat on Aunt Bella's forehead and how she constantly dabbed her face, despite the coolness of the room – just like Dad before his stroke. But I tried not to think the worst.

I reached for Aunt Bella's hand. "Are you alright, Aunt Bella? I've been worried about you."

"Oh, I'm absolutely fine," she said. "I just need to get a few things sorted. The clock is ticking, and all that."

"Why is the clock ticking?" I asked, my chest tightening with worry.

"Oh, nothing. I just like to get things sorted. You know me, Gracey. I'm going to the loo now, and then let's get you home."

While Aunt Bella disappeared to the loo, I took the opportunity to open both parcels. The first, from Rebecca, held a beautifully handcrafted frame containing a photo of the two of us. But when I unwrapped the second parcel, my heart sank with a mixture of sadness and love. Inside was a stunning silver necklace, its pendant in the shape of a heart. Attached was a note that read:

> You're not a butterfly easily crushed and captured. I have never stopped thinking about you. I know you hate me, but I'll never stop loving you. You have a special way with words that truly connects with people. As an editor, you'll only be sharing others' words. The world needs to see yours. Tina xx

I looked down at my butterfly tattoo. *I wish I could speak to you again, Mum.*

"Right, are we ready?" Aunt Bella said when she returned.

I took a deep breath. "Yes, I'm ready."

26

BELLA HOLTON

MAY 2017

I lugged the cat carrier by my side as Margaret and I made our way to the sanctuary. My arms were aching, but I'd never let her know that.

"Grace asked about that photo again." I sighed. "You know, the one I've kept in the kitchen from when the girls were still young? Emma's in the background."

"Oh dear, she's not letting it go, is she?" Margaret replied, her voice gentle. "Maybe it's time they knew the truth?"

The words hit me hard. "Those poor girls have been through so much already. Maybe some things should stay in the past." I paused, thinking it over. "I'll give the photo to James and let him decide."

"That's a good plan." She nodded. "How are James, Grace, and Melody settling in?"

"Grace is doing her best, always trying to be helpful, but I keep reminding her to pace herself like the doctor said." I shook my head, thinking about it all. "Melody, though – poor girl – she's wrapped up in a blanket, staring blankly at the TV. But James..." I chuckled. "James has been smiling a lot at his phone. I swear he's met someone at the hospital. There's no stopping that one."

We finally reached the cats' area. Relieved, I set the carrier down with a huff and knelt in front of one of the apartments. Pickles lay inside, stretched out on her cushion, her green eyes lazily following my movements.

"James deserves someone better than Emma, that's for sure," I muttered as I reached in to lift Pickles out. "And I hope Frank gets the truth from Lilly soon. I don't understand these young ones, Margaret," I said, still wrangling with Pickles. "They can't seem to keep their undergarments on."

Margaret laughed. "My undergarments were always glued on," she huffed, folding her arms.

I laughed as Pickles let out a loud, defiant meow, squirming out of my arms. Just as I scooped her up, Pickles jumped from my hands, her sharp claws catching in my long white hair. The little devil clung on like a furry black hat, claws digging into my scalp. I winced, feeling their sharp sting.

"Flipping heck, Pickles!" I grimaced, trying to keep my balance as Margaret reached over, pulling the carrier aside. She knelt beside me and started stroking Pickles' soft fur. The purring soothed me, but the blasted cat still wouldn't let go of my hair.

"Well, this will be fun." I laughed, leaning my back against the wall, my head throbbing from the claws.

"I was thinking the same thing." Margaret chuckled. "But don't worry, we'll manage it, just like we always do."

Birds tweeted from nearby trees, and Pickles' ears twitched, her whole body tensing in response. Her jaw vibrated as she began mimicking the birds' cries, her little hunter instincts coming alive.

"Margaret, hold on to her!" I warned, but it was too late.

With one quick leap, Pickles sprang free, shooting over Margaret's head and darting through the open entrance.

"Fiddlesticks!" I shouted, scrambling to my feet, my knees protesting as I rushed after her.

Margaret was right behind me. "Pickles, come back!"

Before we could get far, a familiar voice stopped us. "Did you lose a cat?"

Charles stood in front of us, cradling a disgruntled Pickles in his arms. A mixture of relief and embarrassment washed over me as I walked towards him.

"Our hero," I said, taking Pickles from him. Bending down, I slipped the cat into the carrier.

"Charles, how lovely to see you," I said.

"Let me help this damsel in distress to her feet." Charles offered his extended arm.

With his help, I managed to stand, grateful for the support. Margaret hurried over, bringing a fold-up chair for me, and she and Charles held it steady as I plopped down with a sigh.

"Everything OK with your family in Scotland?" I asked, trying to distract myself from the ache in my bones.

"I came back yesterday," he replied. "There's always some family drama, but everyone at the community centre misses you, Bella."

"Can we go inside? I need to speak to you both," I said, feeling the weight of the conversation ahead.

We followed Charles into the living room, my heart heavy with what I had to tell them.

Once we were all seated on the sofa, the silence seemed to stretch on. I took a deep breath, preparing myself.

"We are all looking forward to seeing Fish, Chips, and Mushy Peas next week at the Whitebridge Sands summer fair," Charles said, trying to lighten the mood with a wink at

Margaret. I noticed her grin spreading wide, showing off every one of her false teeth. It was a small comfort in the moment.

"The thing is," I began, "I'm not sure if the band will be able to play next week, seeing as I'm not feeling quite myself. Margaret. I've told you time and time again, you'll be absolutely fine on your own," I added, wagging my finger at her. "It's end of discussion, dear."

I could see the hesitation in her eyes. I knew she didn't feel ready to go on without me.

"It's not as if I'm a member, I'm just your manager."

Her own family had turned their back on her because she didn't fit the image of a traditional grandma, and I'd become her rock. I feared she was relying on me more than she should, especially now that my time was running short.

"I'll be back soon, Charles," I promised. "But this cat sanctuary business, it's left us in such a mess. Frank and Melody were supposed to take care of everything, but then that awful woman...she's gone and ruined it all." My chest tightened, and I instinctively placed a hand over my heart, feeling the familiar flush of pain.

Margaret reached over, resting her hand on my shoulder. "It's alright, Bella. Take a deep breath. I'm sure they'll work it out. Melody just needs some space. You know how overwhelmed she gets."

"I know." I sighed, trying to calm myself. "But she's got a commitment to us too, and I'm cross with Frank. This mess is beyond me. When you meet the right one, it's supposed to be simple, like me and Jim. We never looked at anyone else."

As soon as the words left my mouth, I could see the flash of pain in Margaret's eyes. It hit me like a tonne of bricks.

"I'm sorry, Margaret," I murmured, feeling foolish for my thoughtless words.

Margaret wiped at her eyes with a handkerchief, offering me a faint smile. "It's alright, Bella. Your relationship with Jim was rare. Most of us aren't that lucky."

She was right. I had been so fortunate with Jim, but I often forgot that not everyone had found the love I had. I reached out and gently squeezed her hand.

"Maybe we could ask some of the other volunteers to do more hours while Melody and Frank sort themselves out?" she suggested hopefully.

"That's a good idea," Charles chimed in. "I'm happy to help however I can."

I took a deep breath, knowing it was now or never. "I've made up my mind," I said quietly. "I'm not going to put myself through any more treatment. I want to spend my remaining time with dignity, not stuck in hospitals chasing false hopes."

Margaret's voice trembled as she spoke. "But Bella, you can't give up like this. There are new treatments all the time. We might find something that works. I can't bear the thought of losing you."

Charles took my hand in his, and I could feel the warmth of his support. "Margaret, I don't want to lose her either," he said softly. "But this is Bella's choice. We have to respect that."

"Respect it? How can I respect it when it feels like she's giving up on us?" Margaret's voice cracked, her tears flowing freely.

I turned to her, my heart aching for the pain I was causing. "Oh, Margaret," I whispered. "This isn't about giving up; it's about making peace. I've thought about it long and hard.

I want to join Jim, and I want my final days to be filled with love and laughter, not pain."

Charles nodded beside me. "She's right, Margaret. And you know there's something else. Bella, you need to tell Melody, Grace, and Frank. They deserve to know and spend time with you. They need to hear it from you."

"They'll be devastated, just like us," Margaret added, her voice barely above a whisper.

"I know, but my main concern is making sure they're looked after once I'm gone."

Margaret nodded, wiping her eyes again. "I don't know if I can do this," she whispered, "but if it's what you truly want, I'll try. For you."

I reached out and gently held her hand. "Thank you, Margaret. That means the world to me. We'll face this together, just like we always have."

Charles squeezed my other hand. "We're here for you, Bella. Every step of the way."

I smiled through my tears. "I couldn't ask for better friends. Let's make these days count, for all of us."

27

GRACE BRAXTON

MAY 2017

Amused, I watched as Ida bossed poor George around as they prepared to go out.

"We'll be out for the day. Don't want to be late for our activity groups, do we, George?" Ida shoved George's jacket into his arms.

"No, Ida," George huffed.

"Do you both have everything you need?" George asked in my direction.

"Yes, of course they do, George. One of my many skills is organisation." Ida waved off George's concern. "Carers have been this morning, there's food in the fridge, and there are many channels on the TV."

"We will be back before the carers come back tonight. Ta-ra, you two." Ida pushed George out of the door before he even had a chance to put his jacket on.

"My mother has always had a way with words." Dad chuckled.

Sitting on the floor, I continued putting my dad's woollen socks on for him.

For all Ida's faults, I did admire how she had sorted the

living arrangements in such a short period of time. The carers were great, but they had such limited time to do everything, especially in just two calls.

I clambered onto my knees and then pushed myself up with the support of the sofa, gritting my teeth as a spasm of pain shot through my legs.

"I think we need to rethink my care, duckie. I really don't want all this pressure on you. It's making you worse, and that scares me after all the progress you've made," Dad said.

I sat next to him, and although I was still struggling to understand his speech, it was a lot better than it had been. I was gathering the gist, but I had to make sure I concentrated.

"It's OK, Dad. I want to be here for you, especially after everything you have done for me. I am only doing a few bits and bobs."

My dad stared into space for a moment, with a deep frown.

"Dad?"

"Sorry, yes. But you're supposed to be putting your limited energy into your own pacing plan for your physio exercises and goals, not looking after this old man."

"I am just so grateful to have you back, Dad. I was so worried I was never going to see you again."

"They might try to get us down, but they will never defeat us. But you must put your health first. Look what happened to your old dad when he didn't."

He leaned forward gently and kissed me on the forehead.

"I know, I just don't understand how other people manage to do so many things. You know, be productive all the time – how Mum was."

"Oh, duckie, let's not ruin today by talking about your mother. You are not seeing the past for what it really was."

He leaned back on the sofa, briefly closing his eyes as though in pain.

My chest tightened. I wanted to defend my mother and speak about the good she did for us. Yet, it always ended in a hurtful argument.

Dad opened his eyes, as though he'd had a sudden thought. "Have you spoken to Aunt Bella recently? We received a brilliant hamper from her this morning."

"That huge hamper in the hallway brimming with treats is for us?" I asked.

"Yes, and what made it even better is that the card said, 'Dear James, Gracey, and Melody, in case Ida isn't feeding you properly.'"

We both broke into laughter.

"I can just imagine Ida's reaction. I'll give Aunt Bella a call now," I said.

As I made my way to the living room door, I noticed Dad had quickly got his phone out and was smiling at it again.

"Dad, why do you keep smiling at your phone?" I asked.

"Let's just say I thought I would never have a chance at love again, but there was one positive thing from me being in hospital. Now go have your phone call – your crutches won't be able to hold the extra weight of your huge grin."

I decided to lie down for a quick nap, and as soon as my body lay on my comfortable memory foam mattress, I sighed with relief as the pressure was taken from my legs, like heavy bricks being removed from my limbs. Next to me, Melody was still on her bed, out cold from crying most of the night, her earbuds still attached.

Living together again reminded me of when we were

kids. Then, she would hang on to me for dear life, and I would wake up with my pyjama top covered in her tears. She'd always struggled with her emotions.

Whenever we spoke about our childhood, she always went on about how awful it was because we had an alcoholic mother and a dad absent for long periods. It wasn't easy, but as I kept saying to Melody, our mother was a hardworking journalist who needed a release, and Dad was working around the country all the time. We were luckier than most kids.

This memory made me think of Tina. Maybe I should have given her more slack, though even with the pressures of being a journalist, there was no excuse for what she had done.

When I woke, I went into the other room to ring Aunt Bella. Taking my phone out of my pocket, I stretched out on the sofa, dialled her number, and rested the phone on my chest with the loudspeaker on.

"Gracey! How are you feeling? I've been trying to ring Melody, but the darn child won't answer my calls. I've spoken to Frank. Frank and Lilly had a shouting match. Turns out the hussy doesn't know who the father is and wanted to play Frank and Mrs Holloway's grandson against each other for what she could get."

"You're joking!"

"Margaret! Mr Fluffy is trying to swing from the ceiling fan again," Aunt Bella shouted at Margaret in the background.

"And they won't be able to find out till the baby is born?" I asked.

"No, not without risking harm to the baby."

"Wow, this is huge. How is Frank taking this?"

"Margaret! How will switching the fan on help? We're going to have a splattered Mr Fluffy."

I heard Margaret's response. "It's only on a low speed, Bella."

Aunt Bella brought her attention back to me. "Frank's not good, Gracey. He needs to be in contact with Melody as soon as possible. Will you help persuade her, please?"

"Yes, I'll do my best."

Aunt Bella let out a staggered breath.

"Aunt Bella, are you OK? Do you need the doctor?"

"You're a worrier, Gracey. I'm fine. I just need to sit down. I've got old bones. I'll call you later."

"Before you go, thank you so much for our hamper."

"You're all welcome. Please look after yourself. You can't pour from an empty teapot."

"He has landed on my breasts, Bella. Good job I was wearing a bra, otherwise he would have dropped straight to the floor," I heard Margaret broadcast in the background.

Chuckling at the image, I finished the call.

28

MELODY BRAXTON

MAY 2017

I'd received a message from Frank:

> Babycakes, please pick up. I really need to speak to
> you, it's urgent. I don't want to tell you over a
> message.

All my muscles tightened, and my entire body felt like a
kettle about to boil. I threw my phone across the living room
with force, making a slight dent in the wall, screaming, "I
hate you, Frank!"

Tears welled up in my eyes. Annoyed, I wiped them
away. I wasn't going to cry over that cruel man anymore. It
was such a stupid message, trying to get me to call, as if I
would believe that. I went to collect my phone.

Ida stormed into the room and pointed at the dent.
"What's that on my wall, Melody Braxton?"

"I'm sorry, it's just Frank messaged me, and I got so
angry." My voice started to tremble.

George walked into the room with his newspaper. He sat
in his armchair and hid behind the newsprint.

"Melody, come on, we need to start getting on with things. Life didn't work out as you planned, but now you need to plan a new life. Look at your grandfather. He originally thought his life would be with flashy Barbara in Kent, running a bakery together. When it didn't work out, his heart was broken, but then he met me, and he's lived happily ever since, haven't you, George?" Ida looked at him.

"Yes, dear," he mumbled.

"I'm not ready. I'm just going to stay here for a while, and my dad said he would support me." I folded my arms, staring at the ground.

"You can stay here as long as you like, Melody. Ida, I thought we were going to do better by our son and grandchildren," George said from behind the paper.

Ida grabbed his newspaper and threw it on the floor.

"George! Yes, we are doing our best, and in life, the best support is the hard truth." Turning back to me, she asked, "And how in the world is your father going to support you? He loves both of you girls, but you need to be realistic. He needs to help himself now, and I haven't seen you help him at all. Your disabled sister has been doing that!"

I turned to look at Ida's judgemental face. My legs tapped like crazy.

"You can't see my illness, so you don't think it's there, but I'm struggling just as much as Grace is."

"Yet, Grace is still helping your father. And as much as I disapprove of Bella, you made a commitment to her cat sanctuary, and you just abandoned it."

"I'm always seen as the bad guy! Why can't I just be given a fucking break?"

I rushed out of the room, tears streaming down my face.

"No swearing in this household!" Ida shouted after me.

Slamming the bedroom door, I began banging my head with a soft thud on the wood.

"It's not fair! I need to sit still; it's too much to keep going all the time. They just don't get it. I mean, what sort of stress do they experience? Nothing, that's what," I shouted.

"Grace?" I turned around when I heard no reply.

Grace was curled up, holding tightly onto a pillow. She looked so pale and delicate, with sweat dripping from her forehead.

I took a deep breath and knelt beside her, placing my hand on her arm. She jumped as if she'd been in some sort of trance.

"Gracey, can I get you anything?"

"I'm trying to spread out my last lot of pain relief, but the pain is unbearable. I can't go back to how I was before, Mel. I just can't."

"Still no word from that consultant or your complaint letters to the surgery?"

"No, nothing."

Grace's body shook with violent tears. The groans of distress were unlike anything I'd ever heard before – piercing and heartbreaking. I wrapped her in my arms, trying to steady her trembling body.

"When I saw Patrick yesterday, he gave me a twenty sack of weed, and I've some saved, which is more than enough to help you and me. Listen, I know you've always been dead against it, but I've heard it helps lots of people with pain."

I loosened my arms and faced Grace's hesitant eyes.

"Did you have to give Patrick money for the weed?"

"No, I gave him something else last night." I swallowed down the guilt.

"Please be careful, Mel."

Grace squeezed my hand tightly.

"We won't be able to smoke it in here, but I'll get your wheelchair, take you to my car, and we can hotbox."

"Yes, please," she whispered.

I never thought in a million years I'd be smoking a joint with my sister. My sister, who was very anti-drugs and alcohol, who believed that your career and achievements were everything in life. I would be happy if it were because Grace was starting to let go and have fun, but no, it was because we both knew we'd run out of other options.

Panicking, I stood beside Dad, who was being admonished by the on-duty doctor.

"How long has your daughter been a drug addict, Mr Braxton? You'll find her in Bed 3 on Ward Madeline." The doctor stood in front of us, holding Grace's file.

"Excuse me? This is the first time she's taken an illegal substance." Dad began shaking, and George supported him to sit down.

"Hmm. I see she's being weaned off Oramorph due to concerns of long-term dependence." The doctor's tone was sharp. "The toxicology screen suggests she was exposed to a very strong opioid in addition to her prescribed morphine. That combination could have stopped her breathing."

Dad tried to rise again on his unsteady legs, only staying upright thanks to George's support.

"My Grace is not addicted!" he declared, venom in his eyes.

My heart was racing, but my family needed me. I stood my ground and said, "The only reason my sister took weed is because that awful doctor is taking away her pain relief. The pain relief was helping her."

"She does not need those medications in their current doses," the doctor said. "Miss Braxton will be referred to a drug addiction service as well as pain management support. She's lucky we gave her naloxone quickly — it reversed the opioid in her system."

I wrapped my hair bobbles so tight around my wrist that I cut off the blood flow.

"So, you're just another so-called medical professional who claims to care about their patients, but judges them instead?"

"We do not tolerate abuse in this hospital."

"Melody!" Ida scolded.

"Mum, Melody is right. Grace has been continually gaslit by health and medical professionals when they're supposed to be helping her," Dad said.

"So how did she get opioid poisoning, then?" Ida spat.

"Because that weed must have been laced! I got some weed from my ex, and he must have got it from a dodgy dealer or something. Grace smoked the weed from the new batch, and I smoked the remains of another batch. She was in so much pain, and I gave her far too much for her first time."

"Mum, we need your help here. Please don't close us off again just because we don't fit into neat, perfect boxes."

"Do not speak to me like that, James. Your father and I are doing our best to support you, and this is how you treat us."

"You have my help, son, with or without your mother's," George said, putting his arms around Dad.

Ida's normally confident bravado quickly disappeared. "I am sorry, Doctor, my family have obviously lost their minds," she said and stormed out of the room.

"Doctor, the way you have spoken about my grand-daughter is disgusting. Please tell the manager of your ward to speak to me immediately," George demanded. "And if this is not resolved, I will involve the full extent of the law. We have plenty of evidence to show that Grace is just trying to get her life back, and people like you are just making life miserable for her."

"I will not tolerate any further abuse. If you don't all leave, I will call security to have you removed."

"Do as you like; we are not leaving until we've seen my sister!" I said.

The doctor walked away.

As a family unit, with George and me supporting Dad, we walked to Grace's ward. A nurse was changing the bed where Grace was supposed to be resting. There were no belongings on the side, and a strong whiff of disinfectant hit me.

"Excuse me, where is Grace Braxton?" I asked.

"She discharged herself," the nurse said, continuing to make the bed without looking up.

"What? What are you talking about!" Dad's eyes widened.

"We told her it was a bad idea. She was obviously too unwell. But she has mental capacity, so it's her decision at the end of the day. We can only advise." The nurse shrugged her shoulders.

"So, you just let her go? You didn't think of calling her next of kin or anyone? Knowing she's at risk." I placed my hands on the bed, demanding attention.

"She's an adult, has full mental capacity – it's not our job," the nurse said, fluffing the pillows.

"Did she give any indication of where she was going?" George asked.

"No. Now, I have a job to do." The nurse started cleaning the next bed.

Dad tried not to cry, but he shook and the tears in his eyes were hard to miss.

All I wanted to do was to hide and pretend all this wasn't happening.

When we were back home, George rushed through all the rooms of the house, calling, "Grace? Are you here?" Each door crashed into the wall as he entered.

"No answer on her phone." Dad was phoning everyone he could think of.

"Zoey, her old carer, hasn't heard from her. But she's going to keep an eye out," Dad said.

"I've called Frank and Aunt Bella, but they haven't heard from her either. They asked you to call them as soon as you've found her. They need to tell you about something urgent as well. They wouldn't say what it was. They offered to come down and help, but I think we can handle it for now, plus they need to stay there in case she's travelled down to them."

"Yeah, we don't need them, Dad," I said.

How low can you go, trying to use that line again, especially when my sister is missing? I really didn't know Frank at all.

"Who else can we call? Where could she be?" George asked, wringing his hands.

"I know someone. I don't have her number, but I bet I could call her through Facebook," I said.

There was barely one ring before the call was answered.

"Tina?"

"Melody, hi. Are you OK?"

"I wasn't sure if you'd remember me. I'm Grace's sister."

"Yes, I remember."

"Is Grace with you by any chance, or has she been in touch?"

"No, we haven't spoken for a while, which I know is all my fault. I really miss her."

My chest tightened as my tears began to flow.

"I'm really worried, Tina," I whispered, barely audible.

I knew Grace wouldn't be pleased, but I told Tina what had happened. Something in her caring tone made it easier to talk.

"Oh my god! I wish I wasn't so far away. It's going to take me a long time to get to you, but I'll look at train times and see when the next one is. It will probably be tomorrow, sadly. Maybe check places that were special to you both?"

"We did enjoy going to the local library as kids; we loved it there." I took several deep breaths.

"Great place to start. Message me your address and keep me updated."

29
TINA GILES
MAY 2017

I placed the last item into my suitcase and zipped it up with trembling hands. My phone vibrated on the bed, Melody's name flashing on the screen to confirm the address. Though there was still nothing from Grace. I sighed, swallowing the familiar sting of disappointment.

The train wasn't due for another few hours, but I had one more stop to make before I could think about leaving. My solicitor's office.

Grabbing my bag, I mentally prepared myself for the meeting. This wasn't just about legal battles: it was about my mother, about justice, about the failure of a system that was supposed to care for her.

My feet felt heavy as I walked into the office, the receptionist giving me a sympathetic smile that only made me feel worse.

I was led into a small, stuffy room where Mr Harding was waiting. He looked at me with the same practised empathy he had every time we met. I knew what he was going to say before he even opened his mouth.

"I'm sorry, Tina. We've explored every avenue possible. I'm afraid we can't fight this anymore." His voice was soft, gentle, like he was breaking bad news to a child.

"What do you mean, we can't fight this anymore?" I spat, my anger rising. "They murdered my mother, Harding! They left her suffering, ignored her pleas for help, and now she's dead! And you're telling me to move on?"

He sighed, his shoulders slumping. "I know this is hard."

"Hard?" My voice cracked. "My mother is six feet under because those doctors didn't care. I saved every penny for this. I did everything I could. And now you're telling me they just...win?"

There was nothing more to say. I stormed out of his office, my vision blurred. Rage pulsed through me like electricity, guiding my feet to the place I had sworn I'd never return: my mother's doctor's surgery.

When I pushed through the doors, the sterile smell of disinfectant and the hum of idle conversation hit me like a wall. The receptionist barely had time to look up before I slammed my hands down on her desk.

"Are you all happy now?" My voice echoed through the waiting room. People turned to stare, but I didn't care. "You killed my mum. You left her to suffer, and now she's dead, while you all just go on with your lives like nothing happened!"

I saw the receptionist reach for her phone, probably calling security, but before anything could happen, the doctor stepped into the room. Dr Caldwell. He had known my mother for years, had watched the pain eat away at her. He gestured for me to follow him into his office, away from the stares of strangers.

"Tina," he began as we sat down. His voice was calm; too calm. "I know how much your mother meant to you—"

"Don't." I shook my head. "Don't pretend you care. You let her die."

Dr Caldwell leaned forward, his expression solemn. "Chronic pain is a complex condition, and I wish we could have done more. I truly do. But there's not enough research, not enough funding. In the medical profession, we don't always have the answers. But I know your mum was proud of you, Tina. You did everything you could for her. You took care of her when she needed it most."

I shook my head, unable to hold back the tears anymore. "I wanted to make you all pay for what you did, but I failed."

"You didn't fail," he said softly. "You fought for her. You loved her. She knew that."

The silence that followed was unbearable. I stood up, my legs feeling weak beneath me. Without another word, I left the surgery, walked out of the practice, and made my way to the cemetery.

"I'm sorry, Mum," I whispered as I knelt and placed flowers beside her headstone. "I have to let go of this anger now. I blamed the medical professionals, believed they murdered you by neglect, and I blamed you, thinking you didn't try hard enough. I have to let go of this hatred. It's killing me."

The train was delayed, of course. I sat by the window, staring at my phone, debating whether to send the new version of my article to my editor. My fingers hovered over the Send button, heart pounding as I thought about the consequences of what I was about to do.

Subject: New Article Submission
Confessions of an Undercover Journalist: The True Weight of Chronic Illness

As a journalist, my mission was clear: explore whether chronic illness was an excuse for an easier life. To do this, I joined chronic illness communities on social media, posing as one of them. My own scepticism came from a deep personal wound. My mother took her life after years of struggling with chronic pain. For a long time, I found myself entrenched in legal battles with the local NHS, holding them accountable for her death. This experience left me feeling bitter, and I began to direct some of that anger towards my mother, questioning the legitimacy of her suffering.

At first, I remained detached, taking notes on how the sufferers struggled with everyday tasks, constant appointments, medication routines, and financial strains. I listened to their stories, wondering if their ailments were exaggerated or self-inflicted.

But the deeper I delved, the more I began to see the truth. Chronic illness isn't an excuse – it's a relentless, invisible burden. It tests the limits of human endurance, forcing people to make difficult decisions every day just to function. These individuals aren't escaping responsibilities; they're navigating an existence fraught with uncertainty, where every effort comes at an unseen cost.

Through my investigation, I met someone who shattered all my preconceived notions. She was unlike anyone I had ever known – kind, resilient, with a quiet strength that wasn't immediately visible. Her daily battles, her unwavering courage, opened my eyes. She wasn't escaping life; she was bravely living in a world that many of us can't even begin to comprehend.

Her journey through chronic illness is a heart-breaking testament to resilience in the face of relentless adversity. Despite reaching out to numerous organisations and authorities, she has found little success in navigating her debilitating condition, which causes severe pain and fatigue, often confining her to bed or a wheelchair. The medical gaslighting she faces leaves her feeling unheard and frustrated, as healthcare professionals dismiss her symptoms, attributing them to psychological factors.

It's an ongoing battle. Financial difficulties and social isolation creep in as her illness limits her ability to engage in activities she once loved, and the loss of independence weighs heavily on her, forcing her to lean on others for support. Amid the emotional turmoil of sadness, anger, and despair, she remains determined to seek treatment, be an asset to society, and advocate for herself – illuminating the strength that lies within her journey.

To her and to everyone I deceived, I am deeply sorry. I came into your lives under false pretences, but in the process, I learned a profound truth. Chronic illness isn't a weakness, and it isn't an escape. It's a reality that can't be ignored or diminished.

This article isn't just a confession; it's an apology. To those I sought to expose, I apologise for my ignorance and the harm I've caused. I now see the depth

of your struggles, and I respect the grace with which
you handle them.
To the woman who changed everything: I am sorry
for the deception. I came into your life with the
wrong intentions, but in the process, I fell for who
you truly are. I hope you can find it in your heart to
forgive me.
I love you.

I hit Send.

Just as the train pulled into the station, my phone
buzzed with a new email. It was from my editor:

Are you sure you want to do this? We'll print it
tomorrow.
PS: You're not losing your job.

I smiled for the first time in what felt like forever. I sent her
my answer:

Yes, I'm sure.

30
GRACE BRAXTON
MAY 2017

I sat quietly in the library garden, the same one where Melody and I used to play as children. The bench beneath me was cool, and the scent of lavender filled the air. This place had always been a sanctuary, but now, even the soft sounds of the birds and rustling leaves couldn't soothe the pain gnawing at my body.

I felt as though I was sinking. My body ached in ways words couldn't describe, and the loss of control over my own health had become unbearable. It wasn't just the pain, though that was bad enough, it was the cruelty of the system.

I found myself slipping back into an old memory, one that haunted me more than most.

It was years ago, in this very garden. I was only a child, sitting beside Mum while Melody and Frank ran around, playing weddings. Frank was officiating, and Melody danced around in a veil made from one of Mum's scarves. I remembered how beautiful the day was, how the sunlight had filtered through the leaves, casting soft patterns on the grass.

As they played, I reached for a bottle of fizzy pop next to

Mum. I'd barely touched it when a sharp, acrid smell hit my nose. Mum snatched it away, her lips curling into a lazy smile.

"You can't drink that, Grace. It's got Mum's special medicine in it," she said, taking a long drag from her cigarette and exhaling slowly.

She pulled me closer, lifting me onto her lap. Her movements were unsteady, and I could smell the alcohol on her breath.

"You've always been the special one, Grace. You're like me."

I stared at her, confused, but wanting to believe her. "But Melody's special too, isn't she, Mum?"

Mum's smile faded a little. "Yes, but she's not smart like us. She doesn't have the brainpower we do."

The words left a bitter taste in my mouth, even then. But I stayed silent.

She pointed to the ground where a slug was slowly making its way across the garden path. "See that slug? That's what most people are: slow, dirty, and without purpose."

Before I could say anything, Mum stomped her foot down on the creature, grinding it into the dirt. I flinched, my heart racing as I stared at the smear left behind.

"That's why this happens to them," she said flatly. "Because they don't matter."

I wanted to cry, but I didn't. I just sat there, frozen.

Then she pointed to a butterfly fluttering gracefully in the air. "But we're not slugs, Grace. We're butterflies. Stunning. We fly above everyone else."

The memory faded, leaving me cold inside. I'd carried those words with me for so long, believing them, believing her. But now, sitting in this garden as an adult, I couldn't ignore the truth. I'd got this butterfly metaphor all wrong. Maybe she'd been wrong about everything.

I looked down at my hands, the tremors still faint from the after-effects of the laced weed. My body felt poisoned, but worse than the physical illness was the hollow, aching low I had reached. Sitting there in the library, I couldn't shake the weight pressing down on me. The despair was unbearable, and I kept wondering: *Is this what Melody feels like all the time? Is this the kind of darkness she has been fighting against for so long?*

I glanced down at the bottle of Oramorph sitting next to me on the bench. The random pills I'd pulled from my handbag were scattered next to it. It was all there, laid out in front of me. I could end this. I could make the pain stop. The thought was both terrifying and tempting. I closed my eyes, trying to push the idea away, but it lingered, whispering in the back of my mind.

As I reached for the bottle, something else tumbled out of my bag. A small, worn business card. I stared at it for a moment. It was Amber Levendale's card. We had met months ago at an author talk at this very library. I'd been so excited to finally meet her. My favourite author, whose books had been with me through so many stages of my life. I read them when I was lost, when I was sad, and even when I was happy. Her stories were a constant comfort to me. But what I hadn't expected that day was the revelation that Amber Levendale, the author I had admired since I was young, was also Lucy Perkson, the writer I had once worked with as an assistant editor. Back then, she'd been struggling, and I had tried to help her as best as I could. I didn't realise how much that meant to her until she told me at the event, crediting me with giving her the confidence to keep going as a writer.

At the end of the talk, she'd handed me this business card. No explanation, no offer to reach out, just the card. I'd wanted to contact her before, to thank her for her kindness that day, but I hadn't found the courage. Now, holding the card in my hand, I wasn't sure why she'd given it to me or what I was supposed to do with it. Yet, in that moment, when I felt like I had nowhere to turn, it was the only thing that seemed to make sense.

My hands trembled as I picked up my phone and dialled her number. I hadn't expected her to answer.

"Hello?" replied a warm-sounding voice.

"I don't know why I'm calling," I stammered, my voice barely above a whisper. "I just...I don't know what else to do."

There was a pause, then. "Grace? Is that you?"

"Yeah. It's me," I replied, tears already pooling in my eyes.

"Where are you?"

"I'm at North Litten Library."

"I'm coming. Stay where you are," she said firmly, and before I could argue, she'd hung up.

I sat there, waiting, my mind spinning.

When she arrived, she didn't hesitate. She sat beside me on the bench, took one look at the pills and the Oramorph, and gently took my hands in hers.

"Grace, you're not alone in this. You've never been alone," she said. "I know it feels like everything is closing in, but you're important. Just as you are. You don't have to be perfect, or pain-free, or anything else but yourself."

Her words were like a lifeline. I hadn't realised how badly I needed to hear them until that moment. She didn't stop there. She listened as I explained what had happened. The GP cutting off my pain relief without a second thought; the hospital treating me like I was some addict seeking a fix. Even if I had been an addict, no one should be treated like that. They hadn't cared that I was in agony, that the medication had been the only thing keeping me going.

She made a call, right then and there, to someone she knew at the GP's office.

Within minutes, she had sorted it out.

"You'll get your medication back," she said. "I'll pick it up for you at the pharmacy tomorrow. It'll be OK."

"How did you do it, Amber?"

"Unfortunately, it's more who you know than what you know in this world."

The relief hit me all at once, and I couldn't stop the tears. I hadn't expected anyone to help.

As she comforted me, I heard hurried footsteps. I looked up to see Melody and my dad rushing towards me, panic in their eyes. I hadn't realised how worried they'd been.

"I'm OK," I whispered as they wrapped me in their arms. And for the first time in a long time, I believed it.

Later that evening, Melody, James, George and I sat together in the living room. Ida appeared from the kitchen, looking uncharacteristically apologetic.

"I'm sorry for the way I've been," she began, but before she could continue, George spoke up, his voice stronger than I'd ever heard it.

"I'm not putting up with it anymore, Ida. You've treated us all terribly, and it stops now. If you can't change – or if you can't start treating Grace, Melody, and the rest of us with respect – then this marriage is over."

Ida stood there, stunned, as George's words hung in the

air. I felt a strange sense of pride swelling in my chest. The quiet, reserved George had finally found his voice.

"You have our full support, Grace," he said, turning to me. "You, Melody, your dad...we're all here for you."

The phone rang.

"That will be Aunt Bella again. She has been ringing non-stop," Dad said.

I answered the phone.

"Gracey! Are you OK? You had me worried sick."

"I'm sorry, Aunt Bella. I just couldn't cope anymore. The hospital, the way they treated me. I felt like no one believed me, like I'm just a burden."

"Oh, dearie, you're not a burden. You've been through so much, but disappearing isn't the answer. We need you here."

"Thank you, Aunt Bella. I'm so exhausted. I didn't want to drag everyone down with me."

"You're not dragging anyone down. We love you, Gracey. You're not alone in this."

"Will I see you again soon?"

"Yes, but in the meantime, I'll send you some delicious cake; you need to keep your strength up. You need a dose of vitamin C – how about chocolate orange cake?"

I laughed. "Thank you. See you soon!"

That night, after everything had calmed down, Melody and I went into the living room to relax with a cup of tea.

"You know, Mel, after everything that's happened, I think I understand more than ever what you've been going through with your anxiety and low moods. I'm not saying I know exactly how you feel, but I've always had such a stubborn, ambitious mindset, like nothing could stop me. But this chronic illness, and especially that feeling of complete despair, *has* stopped me lately. It's made me realise how hard it must be for you. I can only imagine what it's like to feel that way all the time."

Melody glanced at me and smiled.

"Thank you. I really appreciate you saying that, Grace. I know how judgemental I've been about your condition in the past. I was frustrated and didn't understand. But I'm trying, really. I hope I've made strides in being better. I just want to keep being a better sister to you."

"You have, Mel. You've come a long way."

"And about the laced weed...I'm so sorry. I didn't know. I would never have given you that if I'd known."

I reached over and squeezed Melody's hand.

"I know. I believe you. We've both made mistakes, but we're still here, right?"

"Yeah, we're still here."

"Love you, sis."

"Love you too, Grace."

Dad interrupted our reconciliation. "There is something I need to tell you. Something about the past."

He pulled out an old photo, explaining that Aunt Bella had sent it to him recently.

"That's Emma," he said, pointing to a woman in the background of the picture. "She was following us."

It turned out to be a night of revelations. Dad told us the whole story, even though it didn't show him off in a good light.

Emma started off as one of his casual hookups, someone he met in a bar because he couldn't stand being around our mum. He was using her, and he made promises he never intended to keep – including disowning us. Before he knew it, Emma had become a more permanent fixture in his life. He even promised that he'd divorce Mum. But then Mum passed, so there was no need for a divorce, and the way was clear for him to marry Emma. He had no excuse not to. But when she got pregnant, he had to admit he didn't want to raise another child. And she was telling the truth – he *did* pressure her into an abortion.

No wonder she was bitter and obsessive.

"I'm sorry," he whispered, tears glistening in his eyes. "For everything I put you through. I would have never disowned you both."

I didn't know what to say, but as Melody squeezed my hand, I realised that nothing needed to be said. We understood each other in that moment. It would take us time to process, but we would get through it as a family.

"Speaking of your mother, I think you've misunderstood the meaning of the butterfly symbol," Dad said. "I know we never talked much about her, and I never really wanted to. But I know how much that symbol means to you."

"Yes, I've been thinking about it a lot lately," I said.

"Your mother saw the butterfly as something free, without responsibility, floating above everyone else. But that's not you, Grace. You're the other side of the butterfly. Beautiful, resilient, and full of hope. And honestly, I think we'll all see that side of the butterfly in our lives soon."

Dad kissed Melody on the temple, then came to me. Warmth radiated through me as though the fog in my mind melted away. It had been there for so long, I almost didn't recognise the clarity that followed.

But just as the weight of the evening began to settle over me, grounding me in a strange peace, my phone buzzed.

A message from Tina. I hesitated, my heart already racing as I opened it.

Attached was an article. My breath caught in my throat. I couldn't believe what I was reading. Then, the doorbell rang.

I opened the door to find Tina standing there. Her eyes

were soft, filled with an unspoken apology. We didn't need words. Instead, she pulled me into a long, silent embrace that said more than anything she could've spoken aloud.

"I've missed you so much," Tina said, her voice heavy with emotion.

Before I could respond, Dad's phone rang, slicing through the tender moment.

We both turned to him. He listened intently, and his face drained of colour. When he finally hung up, he looked straight at Melody, his voice low and shaken.

"Frank's been trying to call you...Milly's gone missing."

31
FRANK HOLTON
MAY 2017

The wind whipped around me, carrying the relentless rain like daggers onto my skin. My boots sank into the wet sand as I stumbled forward, my heart pounding in my chest. James's words echoed in my head: *"Melody's gone to White-bridge Sands to find Milly."* What was she thinking? The storm had come in so fast, and now it was pitch dark, the narrow beam of my torch barely cutting through the rain.

Even the raging weather couldn't numb the grief tearing through me. Aunt Bella. Gone. She'd been the one constant in my life, the pillar I thought would always stand strong. But now, she was with Jim, leaving me behind. *"Pancreatic cancer...diagnosed late...refused treatment."* The doctor's words swirled in my mind, cruel reminders of the truth I didn't want to face.

Tears blurred my vision, mixing with the rain. She hadn't told me. Margaret's wails of despair still rang in my ears. "She didn't want to worry you or the girls," she'd said, as if that made it easier to bear. As if that could fill the hole Bella had left.

I stumbled, barely catching myself as my feet slipped on

the shifting sand. The beach huts came into view, their once bright colours now faded, just like the memories they held. I blinked against the rain, my breath catching in my throat. Aunt Bella's hut, the place where we had spent so many summers, was bathed in a faint light.

I quickened my pace, pushing against the wind. As I approached, I saw them: Melody and Milly. They were huddled together in the tiny hut, soaking wet, shivering from the cold. Relief and heartbreak washed over me in equal measure.

I pushed open the door, the wind howling in behind me as I quickly shut it again to trap what little warmth there was.

"Mel…" My voice was barely a whisper. I shrugged off my jacket, wrapping it around her shoulders. She was freezing, her skin pale. Her drenched hair clung to her face.

"Frank…" she murmured, her voice shaky, but I could hear the raw emotion behind it. She held Milly close, her hands trembling. I sat beside her on the worn-out plastic boxes that used to hold our beach toys, now abandoned like everything else.

"I'm so sorry," I said. "About Lilly, about everything. I don't feel anything for her. I never did. My heart's always been yours."

She looked up at me, her eyes wide. "I thought I lost you, Frank. When I saw you with her, it was like my heart stopped."

I shook my head, tears stinging my eyes. "You didn't lose me. I'm here, babycakes. I've always been here."

There was a long pause, the sound of the wind and rain filling the silence between us. Then, her voice, so quiet, barely audible. "I saw Patrick again. I'm so sorry, that's how I got the weed."

Her words hit me like a punch to the gut, but I stayed still.

She continued. "We...we slept together. It was a mistake. I was so lost, and I didn't know what to do."

I swallowed hard, trying to process what she'd just said. Patrick. I'd always known he was poison. But this hurt. It hurt like hell. But I couldn't lose her. Not now. Not after everything.

"I don't know what to say..." I started, my voice cracking. "But if we're going to make this work, we leave the past behind us. That includes Patrick. And Lilly, we'll handle it better, especially if...if there's a baby involved." My voice faltered at the thought, but I had to stay strong. For her.

She nodded, tears slipping down her cheeks. "I don't know how I'll cope if...if Lilly's child is yours."

"We'll get through it," I said, though the words felt hollow. But we had to believe it.

"Together."

The silence grew between us, thick and suffocating, until I took a deep breath and said the words I'd been dreading. "Aunt Bella's gone. She's dead."

The weight of it hit us both at the same time. I could see the pain flash in her eyes before she crumpled, her sobs breaking through the thin veil of composure she'd been holding on to. I pulled her close, holding her as tightly as I could, feeling my own tears spilling over.

"I can't believe it," she whispered. "Grace! How's Grace going to handle this? After everything she's been through?"

I didn't have an answer. I just held her tighter, Milly nestled between us, her little body warm against the cold.

I looked around the faded hut, worn down by time and weather, yet still standing, just like us. Even in our pain, we were still here. Melody. Me. Milly. Still breathing. Still loving.

235

"We'll take care of Grace," I whispered into Melody's rain-matted hair. "And we'll take care of each other. That's what Bella would've wanted."

We sat there for what felt like hours, the storm raging outside while our own storm raged within. But the thought of Aunt Bella's sanctuary, and everything she built with love, gave me the strength to believe in something beyond this moment. Beyond the pain.

32
FRANK
MAY 2017

Dear Frank,

I'm so sorry I never told you about my diagnosis. I should have, but the truth is, by the time they found it, it was already too late. I didn't want to spend the little time I had left feeling worse than I had to. The treatments would've made me sick, weak, and you know me, I don't like being fussed over. I wanted to go on my terms, with dignity. I miss my Jim so much; he has been gone a long time now, and I'm ready to be with him again.

Son, I've always thought of you as the son I never had. I know I told you that a few times, but I don't think you ever realised how much you mean to me. You've made me so proud in everything you do. But I worry for you. Your parents, they loved you in their own way. But their obsession – the hotel, their work – it consumed them, and it hurt you. I know it did. Please don't follow that same path. Don't let it swallow you whole. I've spoken to Maria, and she's a good worker. I've given her a new contract with more responsibilities and a well-deserved pay rise. I need you to allow this. Promise me you'll take a step back from the hotel before it's too late.

I've left everything to you. All the legal documents are enclosed, and letters to loved ones, but there are a few specific things I need you to do. First, give your home to Grace. You know she's been through so much, and if she doesn't have to worry about paying rent, it'll give her a bit of breathing room. There's enough money in my will to make any adjustments she might need for her health, and I've done my research. Margaret and I spent hours on it. It's a small way of easing the burden she shouldn't have to carry. It's awful how people like her, who can't work through no fault of their own, are expected to live off Universal Credit and PIP, which are barely enough. And if you need care? They take it away. It's wrong, son, but at least we can do this for her.

You and Melody will have my home. It's worth more than yours, so don't think you're losing anything. But please, let Margaret stay in her room. She's no trouble, and she might need a little comfort at first, but she'll be alright. I've come to love her like family, and I know she'll manage just fine with a little kindness from you both.

And Melody, I want her to take over the sanctuary. Margaret will guide her, and with your support, Melody will bloom. She has such a special way with the cats, doesn't she? There's more money in the will to help with her therapy. I know she had a break with everything that happened, but she'll come through this. She has so much potential, Frank. I know you two are meant to be, no matter what the future holds.

As for Grace, encourage her to write. The world needs to hear her words, and I know she feels beaten down by her health, but she's got a gift. Even if it takes time, she'll get there. Remind her of those short stories she did for the sanctuary's social media; those were wonderful and brought us so many fans and donations. She has so much to give, and the world will be better for it.

And you, my dear Frank, take those beautiful photos of yours! I know the hotel's always been on your mind, but you have a passion that shouldn't be left on the shelf. Life is so very short. Follow your passion.

I will always be with you. You've been my joy, my family, and I love you with all my heart.

With all my love,

Aunt Bella

PS: If Margaret wants my fabulous outfits, just make sure she doesn't get her glitter or nail polish on them. You know how she loves her rock 'n' roll look, but my clothes deserve better than that!

Watching the sun break through the clouds outside, I folded the letter slowly, holding it close to my heart. In that moment, I heard her voice. That warm, melodic chuckle. Her footsteps in the hallway. The way she called us all *my darlings,* as if we truly were her children.

A gust of wind passed through the house, rustling the curtains. I smiled through tears.

Somehow, I knew she was still here, woven into every

laugh, every cat's purr, every kindness passed from one hand to another. Aunt Bella hadn't just left us something to remember her by. She'd left us a future.

33

GRACE BRAXTON

SIX MONTHS LATER

"I'm sorry for everything you've gone through, Grace," Dr Finlay said. "We truly let you down."

Dr Finlay had got back in touch with me after a long period of radio silence. I'd come to expect this from the NHS, but it hurt even more coming from someone I'd entrusted with my hopes for future happiness.

But when the doctor explained the reason for the ghosting, I couldn't be mad. If anyone understood sickness and recovery, it was me.

"I want you to know, I'm not going to leave you in the lurch again. I promise."

I accepted the reassurance with the quiet hope that this time, things would be different.

Thank goodness for Amber Levendale, who'd come to my aid in my time of need. She was the reason I was able to keep my medication.

Dr Finlay explained that although long-term medication use had its risks, he wanted to support me with a more holistic and realistic plan for managing my chronic pain – one that centred around *me*, not a textbook. He suggested referring me to a local multidisciplinary pain management team, where I could try a blend of pacing support, occupational therapy, adapted physiotherapy, and gentle body-based techniques. He also mentioned mindfulness-based cognitive strategies – not as a fix, but as a way to help me live beside the pain instead of constantly fighting it. And nothing would be forced. My choices mattered.

"This won't mean abandoning what's already helping," he reassured me. "It's about building something *with* you, not *for* you."

A breath I didn't even realise I'd been holding escaped my lungs. "I feel positive," I said honestly. "It's good to have your support again, and I'm looking forward to exploring new options."

Melody drove us home from the appointment, her soft humming filling the car.

"How are you feeling?" she asked.

"I feel optimistic after talking to Dr Finlay."

"That's great!" she said brightly. I could see the relief in her eyes. We drove in peace for a while before she spoke up again. "So, Frank isn't the father of Lilly's baby!"

"Thank god," I said. "She can finally leave your life."

Melody nodded, loosening her grip on the steering wheel. "We've been through enough."

"How's your therapy going?" I asked.

"I'm making some progress," she said, "but it's a slow journey. Some days are tougher than others, but I'm sticking with it and trying to stay focused on getting better. It's not easy, but I'm taking it one step at a time."

"You've made fantastic steps, Melody. I'm so proud of you."

Melody beamed.

We moved the conversation away from ourselves and onto something more outward-facing, namely the local support group we'd started for people with chronic illnesses and mental health conditions. The online group we initially tried had been a disaster, filled with trolls and toxic competitiveness. But now, meeting in person with a small, local group – at the lovely home that had unexpectedly become mine – made all the difference. We were building a real community, one where we shared advice, supported each other, and made a tangible impact on one another's lives.

When we pulled into the driveway of what had once been Aunt Bella's home – now Frank, Melody, and Margaret's – I felt a sense of warmth and belonging. Even though I had my own place now, with a personal assistant, this house still felt like a second home.

Tina stood at the door, grinning, a tray of cakes in one hand and the adorable Milly in the other.

"Hello, my darling. I know these cakes will never match your Aunt Bella's, but it's a start. Oh, and Happy Six Months." She leaned in, kissing me softly.

We had been taking it slow; rebuilding trust took time. Yet, plans were in motion for her to move in with me. I couldn't wait to close the distance between us and start building our life together.

Melody, Frank, and I had organised the grand reopening of Aunt Bella's Cat Sanctuary. The November afternoon was cool and crisp, with a grey sky draped over the garden. Fairy lights twinkled along the stone paths, casting a magical glow as they danced in the breeze.

Guests wandered through, bundled in thick jumpers, sipping steaming mugs of hot chocolate, while the cats curled up in their warm, blanket-lined huts. The rich scent of chocolate lingered in the air, mingling with the soft glow of the lights as autumn slowly faded into dusk.

The sanctuary was thriving, and I felt an overwhelming sense of pride for what we had accomplished.

Rebecca caught my eye from across the garden. We hadn't seen each other in person for a while, and the sight of her filled me with joy. She looked healthier, and her smile was genuine.

"Grace!" she said, pulling me into a tight hug. "I'm so proud of you. This place is incredible."

"Thank you," I whispered, trying to hold back the tears. "It's been a team effort. How are you?"

Rebecca stepped back, her eyes twinkling. "I'm settling into my new place. Working on my health goals, taking it day by day, you know? But I'm getting there."

"I'm so happy to hear that," I said, squeezing her hand. "You look amazing."

The evening flowed on, filled with familiar faces. George and Ida had come along to offer their congratulations in their usual quirky way. Dad was there, too, of course, and he'd brought someone to meet us.

After hugging both Melody and me, Dad introduced us to Sue, his new girlfriend, a lovely woman he'd met at the hospital. I'd never seen him look so happy. It was as if a huge weight had been lifted off his shoulders, especially now that his divorce from Emma was final.

I spotted Zoey across the crowd, beaming at me.

"You've come so far, Grace. I knew you could do it."

As I stood to give a speech, I caught a glimpse of all the

people who had been part of my life through the ups and downs. I took a deep breath and began.

"Aunt Bella's Cat Sanctuary started with a simple dream," I said, my voice steady despite the emotion welling up inside me. "Jim built this place for his wife, Bella, who couldn't bear the thought of disabled, elderly, and poorly cats being abandoned. She gave them a loving home, just like she gave so many of us – me, Melody, Frank. A place where we feel safe and loved. Her love and support got us through so much, and it continues to inspire me every day."

The crowd was silent, their attention fixed on me, and I felt the weight of the moment settle in.

"The sanctuary is thriving, thanks to Melody's excellent management, supported by a team of dedicated volunteers – and Margaret's expertise. I handle the social media, creating stories to give the cats unique online personalities, while Frank's professional photos bring them to life and boost our merchandise. But none of this would be possible without the incredible support from all of you. I'm writing a book..."

I continued, surprising even myself with the announcement. "It's about my life, the things we've all been through, the strength we've found. Aunt Bella inspired me to share my story, and I hope it will help others too. Thank you all for being here, and for your support."

There was a loud round of applause, which lifted my soul, giving me a confidence boost as I re-entered the crowd.

"And I want to be the first person to receive a signed copy." I heard a voice behind me.

I turned around and hugged Amber warmly.

"I'm so happy to see you!" I said.

"You, too, Grace. You have inspired my next novel."

"Now, that is a dream come true!"

"We'll catch up later." Amber winked.

Margaret had tears in her eyes as I approached her. Charles kissed her cheek.

"You've made Bella proud, Grace. You've made us all proud," Margaret said.

The evening's entertainment came courtesy of Fish, Chips, and Mushy Peas. Arrayed in Bella's fabulous vintage dresses, Margaret and her band performed a gentle, nostalgic melody that wrapped around the room, calming the energy like a soft embrace.

As the evening wound down, Maria came over to speak to us.

"I'm so glad you made it, Maria," Frank said, hugging her tightly. "Work is important, but not as important as *this*." He gestured to the people around him.

"I wouldn't have missed it for the world, and congratulations on winning yet another amateur photography award," she replied.

"Congratulations, Frank!" I said, and he kissed me on the forehead.

"I can't stay too long. Got a hotel to run, remember?" Maria laughed, then leaned in closer, glancing at Melody's stomach with a wide grin.

"Looks like you'll be needing an assistant soon, Melody—"

I blinked, looking between them in confusion. "Wait, what?" I said.

Frank beamed, wrapping his arms around Melody and me, pulling us close. "You're going to be Auntie Gracey."

The words took a moment to sink in, and then I hugged them both, laughing with pure joy. "The other side of the butterfly."

A NOTE FROM THE AUTHOR

Medical Gaslighting

Many dedicated health, medical, social, care, holistic, and therapeutic professionals support numerous people daily against staggering odds. Yet, some dismiss patients with chronic illnesses and mental health conditions, making them feel as though they are losing their minds. This can drive patients to lose all hope for their future. Such behaviour is both unethical and cruel.

Chronic Pain and the Controversy over Pain Relief Medication

The controversy over pain medication centres on the balance between managing chronic pain and preventing addiction. While some argue that over-prescription has fuelled the opioid crisis, many chronic pain patients rely on these medications to function daily when other methods are not successful. Restricting access can lead to unnecessary suffering for those with legitimate needs. The challenge lies in creating policies that address addiction concerns without neglecting the needs of chronic pain sufferers.

Mental Health

Mental health is a unique journey for each person, shaped by their individual background, emotions, and circumstances. Genetics, environment, and personal history all play a role in this diversity. Different people find solace in different coping mechanisms, highlighting the need for personalised care. This underscores the importance of understanding and supporting each person's distinct mental health experience.

Cards2Warriors

I volunteer with *Cards2Warriors*, a charity that spreads hope and encouragement by sending handwritten cards to people affected by chronic illness. Through their programmes, illness warriors, carers, siblings, and medical professionals receive uplifting messages of support throughout the year. These include the **Warrior Card Swap** (monthly card exchanges between illness warriors), **Happy Mail** (themed and surprise cards sent to the wider community), and **Warriors in Crisis** (short-term extra support for those facing particularly difficult times).

For more information, visit:

https://www.warriorcardswap.com/ and/or
https://www.cards2warriors.org/

Helplines That I Have Found Helpful

Samaritans – **0116 123**
Scope – **0808 800 3333**

ACKNOWLEDGMENTS

To my husband, Roy – My rock and the heart of my world. Thank you for believing in me, even when I was filled with doubt. You've held my hand through every setback, lifted me up when I felt broken, and reminded me of my worth when I lost sight of it. You've stood by me with patience, humour, and love when life felt overwhelming. I'm grateful for everything you are, for the way you love me, support me, and make even the hardest days feel lighter. I truly couldn't do this without you.

Lauren – My cousin, my best friend, my constant. We've walked side by side through every chapter of life – joys, losses, struggles, and laughter. Your friendship is one of the most precious things in my life. I wouldn't be who I am without your unwavering love, loyalty, and support.

Angie – My stepmother, thank you for the warmth and kindness you've shown me. From the very beginning, you welcomed me into your family with an open heart. Your support, especially during difficult times, has meant more to me than I can say.

Louisa – Our paths crossed through a writing group, and I'm so grateful they did. Your intelligence, creativity, and thoughtfulness shine through in everything you do. Our conversations and shared passion for storytelling have enriched my life and inspired me to keep going.

Kelly – Meeting you through the spoonie community was a true blessing. Your heart is one of the kindest I've ever known. You've been a source of comfort, strength, and genuine friendship. You understand in ways many can't, and I cherish the closeness we've built.

Natalie –From our university days to now, you've been a wonderful and trusted friend. I've always valued your honesty, loyalty, and the way we can pick up right where we left off. Your journey into motherhood and the loving family you've created is truly inspiring.

Jayne – Our friendship began at university, and it's one I hold so close to my heart. Thank you for standing by me through so many chapters of life, especially during the darkest times, when I didn't always have the strength to reach out. You are a beautiful person.

Jake – My wonderful stepson, thank you for welcoming me so openly into your world. Your positivity, humour, and support have brought light into my life, and I'm so proud of the person you are.

And to my mentor, **Lis**, whose guidance and wisdom have helped shape not only this book but also me as a writer. Your faith in my work has been a gift, and I am endlessly thankful for the time and energy you've invested in my journey. Beyond that, you've become a wonderful friend, and for that, I am truly grateful.

To my incredible beta readers,

Thank you from the bottom of my heart for the time, thought, and care you've poured into reading my novel.

Each of you brought your own perspective, and I'm so grateful for the blend of expertise, lived experience, and compassion you offered:

Natalie Penny – Thank you for your thoughtful reflections as both a reader and an Occupational Therapist. Your professional lens helped me approach representation with care and authenticity.

Pauline Penny – A fellow spoonie, thank you for your honesty and understanding, and for seeing the heart of this story through the lens of lived experience.

Lauren Marland – Your dual perspective as a cake artist and carer added so much richness, and I'm grateful for the empathy and realism you brought to your feedback.

Kay MacLeod – As a fantasy author, your structural insight and creative instinct were invaluable. Thank you for your sharp eye and kind encouragement.

Denise H. Archilla, MSW – Chronic Illness Coach, Chronic Warrior Coaching – Your compassionate guidance and feedback reminded me of the strength and complexity of our community. I'm so thankful for your support.

Hannah Edwards – As a virtual assistant by profession, your fresh eyes and thoughtful feedback brought valuable clarity and balance to the reading process.

I couldn't have asked for a more thoughtful, generous, and compassionate group of readers.

Each of you has walked with me in your own way, helping me keep faith in this journey. Your encouragement and kindness have shaped not just my writing, but my heart. I am endlessly grateful to have you in my life.

ABOUT THE AUTHOR

I live with my husband, stepson, cat, and dog. I was a carer for my beloved mother, who faced early-onset dementia and a progressive neurological condition. I also worked as an Occupational Therapist specialising in mental health. However, due to my own health decline, I had to step away from my career, a difficult transition that took a toll on my own mental well-being. With the unwavering support and encouragement of my loved ones, I discovered the strength to embrace a new path. Now, as an author, I hope my novels offer readers hope, escapism, awareness, and joy.

Please follow me on social media:

 instagram.com/c.helenauthor
tiktok.com/@c.helenauthor

Printed in Dunstable, United Kingdom

72485873R00150